Hover Car Racer

Also by Matthew Reilly

Ice Station
Temple
Contest
Area 7
Scarecrow

Hover Car Racer: *Crash Course*
Hover Car Racer: *Full Throttle*

Hover Car Racer
PHOTO FINISH

BY MATTHEW REILLY

Illustrated by Pablo Raimondi

Aladdin Paperbacks
New York   London   Toronto   Sydney

This book is a work of fiction. Any references to historical events, real people, or real locales are used fictitiously. Other names, characters, places, and incidents are the product of the author's imagination, and any resemblance to actual events or locales or persons, living or dead, is entirely coincidental.

ALADDIN PAPERBACKS
An imprint of Simon & Schuster Children's Publishing Division
1230 Avenue of the Americas, New York, NY 10020
Text copyright © 2004 by Karanadon Entertainment Pty Ltd.
Illustrations copyright © 2007 by Pablo Raimondi
Text previously published in Australia in 2004 by
Pan Macmillan Australia Pty Limited.
All rights reserved, including the right of
reproduction in whole or in part in any form.
ALADDIN PAPERBACKS and related logo are
registered trademarks of Simon & Schuster, Inc.
Designed by Daniel Roode
The text of this book was set in Sabon.
Manufactured in the United States of America
First Aladdin Paperbacks edition April 2007
2 4 6 8 10 9 7 5 3
Library of Congress Control Number 2006923718
ISBN-13: 978-1-4169-0648-3
ISBN-10: 1-4169-0648-7

For Matt Martin

There are no friends on the racetrack.

Jason Chaser has the need for speed—hyper speed. And with his little brother, the Bug, navigating and spitfire Sally McDuff as his crew chief, the 14-year-old hover car racing phenom is geared up to take the world by storm. And that's just what Jason does when he qualifies for hover car racing's biggest amateur competition, the International Race School's Sponsors' Tournament. But qualifying is just the beginning. Higher stakes means even fiercer competition, and even the closest friends can become bitter adversaries at the starting line. His newfound comrade, American pilot Ariel Piper, is Jason's first challenge, and she is followed by Jason's hometown rival, Barnaby Becker, who still has a few tricks up his sleeve. And once again there's the mysterious driver in black, Prince Xavier Xonora, who just manages to keep Jason out of first place at the tournament. But the fans have the last word. Although the *Argonaut* comes in second place, Jason is hands down their favorite racer. Xavier won the race, but Jason's "never give up, never say die" attitude has won him the hearts of racing fans, along with a professional sponsor and an invitation for Jason to race in his first professional race. School's out! Hopefully Jason has learned his lessons well, because the time for child's play is over—his adult competition is out for blood.

FOR A COMPLETE DESCRIPTION OF THE EVENTS
LEADING UP TO THE START OF THIS BOOK, READ THE
FIRST TWO HOVER CAR RACERS:
CRASH COURSE AND FULL THROTTLE.

Hover Car Racer

PHOTO FINISH

PART I

THE DEATH OF JASON CHASER

THE FINAL STAGES OF THE ITALIAN RUN
VENICE II, ITALY

The explosion of Kamiko Ideki's Yamaha crashing at 435 mph into Jason Chaser's stricken *Argonaut II* echoed across Italy—in every grandstand, in every home, on every television, on every digital radio.

For a full twenty seconds, not a single person in all of Italy spoke.

They just stared at the ghastly scene in horror.

Where once there had been two racing cars, now there was just a rising cloud of black smoke.

No one could believe it.

Were Jason Chaser and his little brother, the Bug—the two young boys from the International Race School who

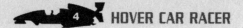

had won the hearts of race fans with their determined, never-say-die attitude, and who had turned the tables on Fabian during that wonderful exhibition race—dead?

Killed in a spectacular blazing inferno?

Watching from a hover stand overlooking the Finish Line, Henry and Martha Chaser were in total shock.

They couldn't move, couldn't breathe, couldn't drag their eyes away from the tall wispy smoke cloud on the water's surface—the smoke cloud that had once been their sons.

"Oh, no . . ." Martha gasped. "Dear God, no!"

Henry just whispered: "Come on, Jason, tell me you got out of there. . . . Please tell me you got out of there. . . ."

But nothing happened. Rescue vehicles took off from the shore, their emergency lights blazing.

They arrived at the smoke cloud just as, without warning, two tiny figures burst up from beneath the surface of the harbor seventy feet away from the big black cloud.

Jason and the Bug!

Henry and Martha leaped to their feet.

The crowd—formerly silenced—now positively *roared* with delight.

The rescue vehicles cut a beeline for the two boys, now bobbing on the surface. Every TV camera in the area zoomed in on them—but on this closer view, the scene took on a disturbing angle.

The Bug was waving frantically, but Jason wasn't moving at all.

Thirty seconds earlier:

The *Argonaut II* lies on the surface of the wide body of water at the end of the Grand Canal, a hundred yards short of the Finish Line. It lies upside down. Jason surfaces, sees Kamiko Ideki's Yamaha heading straight for him. He holds his breath, goes under to save the Bug. Four seconds later, Ideki's Yamaha *slams* into the *Argonaut II*. Boom.

Seen from under the surface of the water, it is a different scene altogether.

Things are happening.

Shoooooooom!

Jason sees that the Bug's seat belt is jammed. It cannot be undone in time—certainly not in enough time for them to get away from the blast zone of the impending crash.

So inside four seconds, Jason does the only thing he can think of.

Straddling the Bug's upside-down seat, effectively sitting on his trapped brother's lap, he yanks on the ejection lever.

Shooooooooom!

A supercharged finger of bubbles lances down and away from the overturned *Argonaut II*—it is the Bug's seat ejecting not upward but *downward* into the blue-green world of the harbor, with both brothers sitting on it—a split second before the *Argonaut II* is hit from above by the Kamikaze and explodes in a burst of roiling bubbles.

The water "catches" the rocketing ejection seat on its downward flight, slows the boys about one hundred feet below the surface.

The Bug is still screaming, blowing bubbles.

Jason has been gripping his seat belt's clasp for the

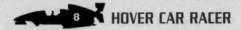

whole of their downward flight and suddenly—*snap!*—it comes free.

The Bug wriggles out from his seat—and sees that Jason isn't moving. He grabs Jason and kicks for the surface, powered by adrenalin, expelling air as he rises. He cannot know that his brother's lungs are filled with water—water that rushed into his open mouth as they plummeted down through the blue haze.

They hit the surface together and the Bug starts waving frantically, trying to get someone, anyone, to come and help his unconscious brother—the brother who risked his life to save his.

Jason dreamed.

As he did so, his mind raced with fleeting images:

Of himself being loaded onto a hover copter—of shouting voices—someone pumping on his chest—flying over Venice II with the sun in his eyes, and then abruptly coughing, vomiting water, expelling it from his lungs . . . and then *breathing*, inhaling and exhaling, wonderful deep breaths of glorious air . . . and then falling fast asleep.

Voices in his dreams:

"He's going to be all right, Mr. Chaser," a man's voice said calmly. "He's just sleeping now. You can go back to the

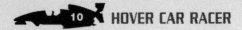

hotel. We'll call you when he regains full consciousness."

"I'm not going anywhere till my son wakes up," Henry Chaser's voice replied.

At one point, Jason woke up briefly, just long enough to see that he was in a bed and wearing pajamas. The bed was in a hospital of some sort and it was the dead of night—moonlight streamed in through a nearby window.

And in that brief instant, he saw his father slouched in a chair under the window, sitting upright but asleep, his chin all bristly and unshaven, his clothes rumpled. They were the same clothes he'd been wearing on race day.

His father hadn't left his bedside.

Jason fell asleep again.

Then the nightmares came.

They all involved crashing a speeding hover car.

Hitting the entry pillars of a mountainside tunnel.

Slamming into a cliff face near the Race School.

And worst of all—in the most often repeated nightmare—

Jason would find himself rushing at the surface of the Grand Canal, his car out of control, his steering wheel completely unresponsive.

And as in all the other nightmares, a nanosecond before he hit the water, his eyes would dart open and he would find himself lying in his bed, breathless, drenched in sweat.

Then, one day, sunshine hit Jason's eyes and he awoke fully.

He opened his eyes to immediately see his father staring at him from his chair, smiling. "Hey there, son."

"Hi, Dad." Jason's throat was dry. He blinked, sat up. "How long have I been asleep?"

"Almost two days now." Henry Chaser checked his watch.

"Two days . . ."

"All of Italy has been waiting to hear that you're okay. You're a hero, saving your brother like you did—while an out-of-control hover car was screaming right at you. I'm very

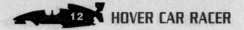

proud of you, son. Very proud. You could have gotten away, but you didn't. You didn't leave your brother behind."

And Henry hugged Jason. Hard. "Good boy."

Half an hour later, Martha Chaser and the Bug rushed into the hospital room, followed by Sally McDuff and Scott Syracuse.

Martha enveloped Jason in a bear hug, as did the Bug, who whispered in his ear.

"No problem, buddy," Jason replied. "You wouldn't have left me."

Sally said, "All right, hero. I tell you, when you lose, you really lose in style. You like going out with a bang, don't you? Although, I have to say, reports of your death have been greatly exaggerated."

She handed him a copy of *Il Corriere Della Sera*, the Italian daily newspaper, headlined "The Death of Jason Chaser" and accompanied by a photo of the *Argonaut II* being hit by Kamiko Ideki's Yamaha and exploding into flames.

Sally explained: "Apparently, the *Corriere Della Sera*

prepared two editions for today's paper—one with you alive, the other with you dead—and they accidentally printed a thousand copies of the wrong edition. I think I'm going to get this framed."

Jason snuffed a laugh.

"How's Mr. Lombardi taking it?" he asked.

"At first he was horrified that you might've died driving one of his cars. But then, when he was informed that you were okay—"

"WHERE IS HE?" a loud voice boomed from the corridor outside Jason's room.

Umberto Lombardi strode into the room, his eyes wide. "Where is the young man *who destroyed my car?*"

Jason shrank into his pillow, not entirely sure if Lombardi was really angry or just faking it.

Lombardi stopped in front of him . . . and his angry face relaxed into a wide mischievous grin. "I just have to know, young Signor Chaser, what does it feel like to *destroy* a thirty million dollar Ferrari?"

"I'm sorry, Mr. Lombardi."

"Bah! Forget it. It's insured—and I love claiming big payouts from insurance companies! God knows I pay them enough in premiums! But you, you're *a hero*, boy! Which means you've made *me* a guy who *employs* heroes. I just hope you don't mind me basking in the reflected light of your magnificent glow!"

"You can bask all you want, sir. I'm still sorry about the car."

"Don't even think about it," Lombardi said kindly. "Ferraris come and go, but young men like you"—he winked—"come once in a lifetime."

But Jason couldn't stop thinking about it.

Nor could he rest.

As soon as he was able to, he asked for a videodisc copy of the final moments of the race and he watched his crash over and over again.

He saw his car overtake Trouveau's Renault—moving into 5th place—then saw it swing around the final left-hand turn, banking under the Accademia Bridge . . .

before, without warning, its tailfin just exploded to nothing.

Then he watched in horror as the black and yellow Ferrari arced down into the water, where it tumbled and splashed and rolled, before it stopped abruptly, upside down.

And then the Yamaha screamed into it.

Boom.

What the hell had happened to his tailfin? he thought. *What had caused it to explode?*

It was just too weird. And since there was nothing left of the *Argonaut II*, it was impossible to inspect the wreckage.

But Jason knew one thing: Tailfins didn't just explode by themselves. Sure, a broken tailfin might get rammed and drop into the airstream of a car's own thrusters, but such instances were rare, and by all appearances, Jason's tailfin hadn't been damaged in any way.

It had just spontaneously exploded.

The truth was clear to Jason: Someone had tampered with his car in order to eliminate him from the Italian Run.

And now, more than anything, he wanted to know who that had been.

• • •

At one point, as he was watching the videodisc for the thousandth time, his mother tapped lightly on the door.

"Hello, dear," Martha Chaser said. "There's someone here who was hoping to see you."

Martha stepped aside—

—to reveal Dido, standing shyly in the corridor behind her.

Jason's face broke out in a wide grin. "H . . . hi," he said.

"I'll leave you two alone," Martha said, walking out.

Dido entered Jason's hospital room tentatively. "How're you feeling?"

Just at the sight of her, Jason felt a lot better.

As Jason regained his strength over the next two days, Scott Syracuse informed him about what had been happening back at the Race School in his absence.

When Jason had come to Italy, he'd been in fourth place in the Race School Championship Standings. During the week of the Italian Run, he'd missed three races. But now, with his hospitalization, he would miss at least one more.

The standings looked like this:

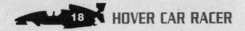

	THE INTERNATIONAL RACE SCHOOL CHAMPIONSHIP STANDINGS AFTER 40 RACES			
	DRIVER	**NO.**	**CAR**	**POINTS**
1.	XONORA, X.	1	*Speed Razor*	266
2.	KRISHNA, V.	31	*Calcutta-IV*	259
3.	WASHINGTON, I.	42	*Black Bullet*	247
4.	BECKER, B.	09	*Devil's Chariot*	240
5.	PIPER, A.	16	*Pied Piper*	235
6.	SCHUMACHER, K.	25	*Blue Lightning*	229
7.	WONG, H.	888	*Little Tokyo*	225
8.	CHASER, J.	55	*Argonaut*	217

Jason was stunned.

Just missing three races had seen him drop from 4th to 8th. Xavier, of course, was still coming in first—he'd been so far ahead when he'd left.

And Jason was well aware that it was only the top four racers who got to participate in the New York Challenger Race at the end of the season.

Investigations would have to wait.

It was time to return to Race School.

• • •

Jason was packing his bags, getting ready to leave his hospital room, when a nurse arrived carrying an envelope.

"This just came for you." She handed him the envelope.

Jason opened it and frowned. It read:

SO? HOW ARE THOSE NIGHTMARES GOING?

RUN BACK TO THE PLAYPEN, LITTLE BOY.

REGARDS,

FABIAN.

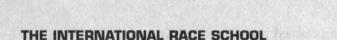

THE INTERNATIONAL RACE SCHOOL
HOBART, TASMANIA

Jason returned to Race School to find that during his short absence, the world certainly hadn't stopped.

Lessons were still going on in classrooms; the pits rippled with practice sessions; cars darted every which way, shooming up the inland highways or whizzing around Storm Bay.

Since he was still barred from racing for two more days, Jason was restricted to classroom work only.

At his first lunchtime back, Ariel Piper sat down beside him.

"Hey! Look who's back!" she exclaimed, clapping him on the shoulder. "The only racer in the world crazy enough to eject *downward*! How're you feeling?"

"Better every day," Jason said. "Can't wait to get back out on the track."

Ariel said, "Hey, thanks again for letting me take on Fabian in that exhibition race. That was very cool of you."

"I thought you deserved the chance to take him down."

Ariel smiled. "Jase. You can't imagine the impact that race has had on me . . . and on a lot of girls around the world. You should see the fan mail I've been receiving. Lot of chicks wanting to be racers. Lot of girls who were thrilled to see Fabian go down. It made an impact. Thanks for the opportunity."

"No problem. I was happy just to get some peace and quiet to practice," Jason said. "Looks like you've been racing well back here too. What are you in the standings now? Fifth?"

"Yuh-huh." Ariel grinned. "One win, one second, and one seventh. Twenty-three points in three races. That race against Fabian gave me my *fire* back. My *desire*. I'm coming in fifth now, and the top four beckons. I wanna go to New York."

Jason nodded, saw the fire in her eyes. The old Ariel was back.

"Good for you," he said.

As he spoke, he looked around the cafeteria and noticed that a few new friendships seemed to have formed in his absence: Horatio Wong was sitting at Barnaby Becker and Xavier Xonora's table. So was the young Mexican driver, Joaquin Cortez. At the moment, Xavier's mentor, Zoroastro, was talking to Wong and Cortez, and the two lesser drivers were listening to him intently, occasionally nodding.

Ariel saw them too. "Yes, hmmm. Zoroastro and Barnaby Becker have been doing a lot of networking while you've been away. *A lot*. They had lunch with Wong and Cortez every day last week. I even saw Zoroastro having dinner with your buddy Isaiah Washington one night."

"What do you think it means?" Jason asked.

Ariel was silent for a moment.

Then she said seriously, "We're coming to the business end of the season. Everything is up for grabs. The championship is on the line. Four places in the New York Challenger Race are there to be won. Races are gonna get harder, too—longer, more challenging, more demanding. And don't forget that the last ten races are run under pro rules—demag strips everywhere, dead zones, driver-over-the-line finishes.

"We're entering a whole new world of racing, Jason, and I think Zoroastro and his boys are creating a few strategic alliances. I get the feeling Race School is about to get very, very serious."

Ariel couldn't have been more right.

The next day, Jason sat in the stands with Sally and the Bug and watched Race 41. It was so frustrating, just watching, but fortunately this would be the last race they'd have to sit out. The doctors had given Jason the all-clear to compete in Race 42.

Sitting with them was one other person: Dido.

It turned out that the last few weeks of the Race School season coincided with her school vacation in Europe, so (at her parents' expense) she had come to Tasmania to support Team *Argonaut*.

True to Ariel's prophecy, Race 41 was a fiercely contested race—Race School had acquired a new level of intensity.

It was also Xavier Xonora's first school race since his impressive fourth-place finish in the Italian Run.

He didn't disappoint.

He won Race 41 convincingly, prompting many to say that racing at the pro level had steeled him, made him an even better racer than he already was—if that were at all possible.

After the race was over, Sally and the Bug headed off to get some dinner, discreetly leaving Jason and Dido alone in the grandstand.

"So," Dido said, "you must be busting to get back out there."

"Yeah, I guess so," Jason said.

Dido turned, surprised. "You're *not* busting to get out there?"

"You wanna know something funny?" Jason said. "I've never been afraid of getting inside a hover car in my life . . . until now."

Dido frowned, but didn't speak.

Jason looked away, biting his lip, as if he was deciding whether or not to reveal more.

He took the plunge.

"Everyone assumes that I'm fearless, Dido. That I'm not afraid of the high speeds, and that I just can't wait to get back out on the racetrack. But I'm not fearless. I never was. It's fear that creates adrenalin and it's adrenalin that makes me a good racer. But right now, I'm scared. Dead scared of getting back in the *Argonaut*."

"What do you mean?"

"Every night I have nightmares, nightmares about my tailfin exploding or some other racer swiping it off during a race, causing me to lose control and crash. Now, I've crashed before, lots of times, but every time I crashed in the past, I knew why. But in Italy, I lost my tailfin for no reason that I can figure out. I lost control and I don't know why.

"I used to love the speed, love racing. But now . . . now I'm not so sure. I'm terrified of getting in that car again, and even more terrified that I'll fail and let my family and my teammates down." He turned to her. "Dido, what happened in Italy changed me. I'm not sure I can be the racer I was before Italy."

Dido looked at him closely.

Then she gently grabbed his hand. "You know, my uncle once told me something about heroes: Heroes are not people who don't get afraid. No. Heroes are people who take action *even when they are afraid*. Don't put too much pressure on yourself, Jason. Take it slowly; one step at a time. And know this. *I* think you can do it."

And with that, she leaned forward quickly and kissed him on the cheek.

Then she dashed off, dancing down the stairs of the grandstand, leaving Jason delightfully stunned by her kiss.

RACE 42 (SUPERSPRINT)
RACETIME: 29 MINS 32 SECONDS
LAP: 29 OF 50

On Lap 29 of Race 42, as they both shot down the southern coastline of Tasmania at full speed, Horatio Wong cut wildly—and inexplicably—across Jason's rear end and smashed clean through his tailfin, blasting it into a thousand pieces and thus causing Jason to lose all control of the *Argonaut*, just like in the Italian Run.

It was loss of control at 500 mph.

That Wong had been *a full lap behind Jason* at the time and completely out of the race made it worse. He should have just made way for the *Argonaut* to pass. Instead he hit Jason square on the tailfin.

Wong flailed away to the left, but pulled up safely in a dead zone.

Jason, however, veered right and down, rushing toward the ocean waves, terrified.

He grappled with his steering wheel, but to no avail. He kicked his thrusters, trying to steer that way—and somehow managed to run the *Argonaut* over a full line of demag lights, thus diminishing its magnetic power.

The *Argonaut*'s power drained fast, and it slowed. A quick burst from its left thruster caused it to fishtail to a skidding halt a bare foot above the waves.

Other cars boomed past it, shaking the air.

The Bug and Sally were shouting in Jason's earpiece—but all Jason could do was sit there, staring forward in shock and swallowing hard.

He looked at his hands.

They were shaking terribly.

When the *Argonaut* returned to the pits, towed by a recovery vehicle, Jason saw Scott Syracuse standing in front of Horatio Wong, letting him have it:

"—what the hell was that! Straight section of track and you suddenly lose control . . . and you take out his tailfin perfectly!"

"I just lost control, sir," Wong shrugged, looking down. "Lost my steering and never saw him there. I can't explain it."

"You just lost control. Lost your steering. Never saw him." Syracuse shook his head with disgust. "I'm not so sure about any of that, Mr. Wong. Get out of my sight."

Wong stalked off, glaring darkly at Syracuse.

Sally came over to Jason, who was still badly shaken.

Jason said, "What's going on?"

"Syracuse just went *ballistic* at Wong for hitting you," Sally whispered.

"But it was an accident," Jason said. "At least, it looked like one."

Sally said, "Syracuse didn't think it was an accident at all. When it happened, he was standing next to me, watching on the monitor. He said it was a classic pro tactic: When a young racer is coming back from a bad accident and his self-confidence is shaky, you hit him in a similar way on his return race—and thus crack his fragile confidence. It's a tactic designed for one purpose: to put a young racer out *for good*."

"But Wong also put himself out of the race by doing it," Jason said, perplexed.

"That's what pissed Syracuse off the most. Wong was the patsy, the junior guy who did the deed and took the fall—someone with pro experience told him to take you out. *That's* why Syracuse was chewing out Wong. He reckons Wong was doing someone else's dirty work."

Jason looked over at the departing Wong, and thought about his new dining companions.

Sally put her arm around his shoulders. "Confidence hits. Geez. Those sort of tricks aren't gonna be a problem with you now, are they? Jason Chaser, Superstar of the Sponsors' Tournament, Hero of Italy, little guy with nerves of pure steel. Like you'd ever have a confidence problem."

Jason didn't reply.

He just hid his shaking hands.

PHOTO FINISH

Jason had two days till he had to race again.

And he was absolutely dreading it.

Whoever had told Wong to take out his tailfin had been smart. Very smart.

Because it had worked.

Going into Race 42, Jason's confidence *had* been wavering, not that he'd dare tell anybody in his team or family. And losing control in exactly the same way as he'd lost it in Italy had totally freaked him out.

He didn't want to tell the Bug or Sally that he was losing it. Didn't want them to think he was somehow a lesser driver. Nor did he want to confide in his parents: They got such a buzz out of his achievements, he didn't want to disappoint them by revealing his fears.

That was the bonus of having Dido around—she was sort of *external*, not a family member or a team member. She didn't have any expectations. She just liked him for who he was.

They met each other for lunch the next day at a coffee shop not far from the Race School.

Jason got there early and was already sitting at a table when Dido arrived.

And then a strange thing happened.

Barnaby Becker walked into the shop at the exact same moment Dido did, and as he stepped up to the takeout counter, he checked her out.

Jason was sitting close enough to hear every word of the ensuing conversation:

Barnaby said, "Hey there, cutie. You're the chickie who's been hanging out with little Chaser, aren't you?"

"Yes, so?" Dido had replied.

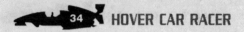

"So. You ever want to go out with a real man, Becker's the name, give me a call."

Dido had snuffed a laugh. "That's a very nice offer, but I don't like *Neanderthals*. I like cultured and courageous young men. Men like Jason. Good-bye."

And with that, she'd spun on her heel with the grace of a ballerina—leaving Barnaby speechless—spotted Jason, and waltzed over.

By the time she sat down, Jason was grinning from ear to ear.

RACE 43

Two days later, Jason was back in the driver's seat for Race 43. If he was going to finish the year in the top four, he needed to finish in the points today.

He ended up finishing seventh, garnering four points, having spent the greater part of the race staying well clear of all the other cars. It was a timid drive—and both the Bug and Sally noticed it.

That said, there was one hairy moment very early in the race: In the hurly-burly of the start, with all the cars jostling for position, Jason could have sworn that Joaquin Cortez had tried to ram his tailfin.

Jason had swerved wide, clipping some demag lights for his trouble, and the two cars had missed each other by inches.

Just racing? Jason thought. *Or was it something more?*

Or was he just getting paranoid?

Either way, he thought, he had to do something about this confidence thing.

The next race was on Tuesday. So he had three whole days to work out a solution.

He started on Sunday morning . . . at 5:30 a.m.

Before first light, he got up and, leaving the Bug fast asleep in his bunk, went down to Pit Lane and, in the silence, pushed the *Argonaut* out of its garage.

He clamped some new mags on her and attached a little hover trailer to her rear hook. Then he jumped in and blasted out of the pits, heading inland, up toward the forested northern end of the island.

And there he ran loops around a course of his own design, a tight winding track around the upper forests and islands of Tasmania.

At first he did his laps alone, just timing himself with the *Argonaut*'s digital stopwatch.

Later, he pulled eight mechanical objects from his hover trailer—hover drones.

Bullet-shaped, superfast, and extremely nimble, hover drones were training tools usually used to train very young hover car drivers, giving them a taste of other racers flying all around them, but without risking anyone's safety, since they were equipped with proximity sensors— meaning they couldn't actually collide with a car. For a racer at the Race School to be using them was like an Olympic swimmer using water wings to swim. They were only at the school for Open Days, when young kids came to race around the school's tracks and get tips from the teachers.

Jason, however, reprogrammed his drones to race the course with him in a hyperaggressive manner, darting and swooping all around the *Argonaut* as it raced—giving him the sensation of closely moving rival cars, *retraining* himself. That said, he still kept their anticollision proximity sensors switched on.

At first the drones whipped across his bow as they raced, cutting dangerously close—then they started zinging across his tailfin, missing it by fractions of an inch.

And Jason drove . . . and drove . . . and drove.

Indeed, he was concentrating so intently that he never noticed the pair of people watching him through digital binoculars from a nearby hilltop.

Monday morning.

And he went up north again and raced alone in the dewy green forests of Tasmania.

This time he disengaged the drones' anticollision sensors, and at one point in his racing, one of the drones bounced hard against his tailfin, denting it, creating a loud bang, shocking Jason.

He immediately pulled to a halt.

He was hyperventilating.

"Don't do that!" he yelled aloud to himself. "Start your car again and get back up there."

He keyed his power switch and flew back out onto his track. Immediately the drones were swarming around him like a pack of killer bees.

Bang! He was hit on the side.

He clenched his teeth, kept driving.

Bang! Again. Other side.

Kept racing.

Bang! This time it was on the tailfin, and the *Argonaut* lurched violently to the side, losing control . . .

. . . but Jason righted her . . .

. . . and regained control.

In his helmet, he breathed again.

And he smiled.

The two people watching him from the hilltop did not.

He was back at his apartment before eight. The Bug was still snoring.

Tuesday morning. Race Day for Race 44.

Again Jason headed north before sunup.

Only this time, when he reached his starting point with his trailer full of drones, two people were already there, waiting for him, the same pair of people who had watched him practice by himself the previous two mornings.

Sally and the Bug.

"Hey there, champ," Sally said, illuminated by the winglights of the *Argonaut*. "Shouldn't you be in bed?"

Jason froze. "I . . . I just wanted to practice on my own. . . ."

"On your own?" Sally frowned. "Why?"

Jason winced. "I just . . . I was . . . I mean—" He sighed. "I've been a wreck ever since the Italian Run, Sally. That crash freaked me out. And then when Wong hit me in my first race back here, I just cracked. I've been coming up here trying to get my nerve back."

"We know," Sally said. "We've been watching you. The first morning you came, the Bug heard you leave. He followed you, to see where you were going, and then he called me. Why didn't you ask us for help?"

Jason shook his head. "I didn't want to let you guys down," he said. "I wanted to figure it out . . . and fix it . . . and I thought . . . I thought that was my responsibility."

Tears began to form in his eyes. He bit his lip to hold them back.

Sally saw this, and she stepped forward.

"You know, I screwed up once, and some little punk gave me some good advice. He said, 'We win as a team, and we lose as a team.' He was right, Jason. We're all in this together. And whether we win or we lose, the members of Team *Argonaut* back each other up. You don't *ever* have to go it alone, Jason. If you've pissed me off in any way by doing this, it's sneaking off and coming up here all by yourself."

"But I have to be the best," Jason said.

"No, you don't," a quiet voice said.

Jason started.

So did Sally.

Because it wasn't Sally who had spoken.

It had been the Bug, standing beside her. It was the first time Jason had ever heard him speak to two people at the same time.

"You don't have to *be* the best. You just have to *do* your best," the Bug said quietly. "If you do your best"—he shrugged—"I'll follow you anywhere, Jason. I love you."

"Me too," Sally affirmed, smiling. "The follow-you-anywhere part, not the love-you part."

And Jason laughed.

"Now then," Sally clapped her hands. "The whole world's against us, our backs are to the wall, and we need to win some races if we're gonna make the top four. But our fearless racer is a little unnerved. The question is, what the hell are we gonna do about it?"

In the end, it was the Bug who came up with the answer.

A quiet voice

RACE 44

Race 44 saw Jason lead from start to finish, the win earn-ing him ten beautiful points in the Championship standings.

That was the Bug's plan.

Win the start—and lead all the way, thereby staying out of range of any would-be assassins—and thus win the darn race. Simple. Then in the days between races, Team *Argonaut* would work together, helping recharge Jason's broken confidence.

It helped that Race 44 had been a Last-Man Drop-Off, meaning that lapped racers (like Horatio Wong in Race 41) hadn't been a problem.

It also helped that Xavier Xonora had sat out Race 44,

choosing to rest, since he was so far out in front of the rest of the field in the Championship standings.

Every morning from that day on, Jason and his team could be found practicing up in the far northern forests of Tasmania from sunup to breakfast time. Then they would return to the Race School and commence their daily classes.

Word got around.

The locals and their families—business owners and workers on the school-owned island—many of whom lived up on the northern islands, would come out onto their balconies with their morning cups of coffee and watch the *Argonaut* get harried by its drones in the light of the rising sun.

Soon the local kids would come out and watch, cheering as the *Argonaut* clashed with its drones.

A series of tiny dents now pockmarked the *Argonaut*'s tailfin. It looked shabby, but as far as Jason was concerned, every dent was another brick in his wall of confidence.

He was rebuilding himself.

He was coming back.

He charged through Race 45 like a demon, coming in third behind Xavier and Barnaby. Eight points.

More early-morning practice.

Race 46 was a gate race, and, guided by a brilliant strategy from the Bug—a course that kept him well away from any assassins—he won, albeit in a tie with Xavier, the two of them ending the race with an equal number of gate points. Ten Championship points.

More early-morning practice.

Then Race 47: win (over Barnaby and Washington in a race that employed the Port Arthur shortcut—the Bug remembered the correct way through; Xavier didn't race).

Race 48: second (to Xavier; in this race, Ariel bowed out with another technical problem, a few of which had started to plague the *Pied Piper* lately).

Race 49: third (behind Krishna and Barnaby; Xavier hadn't even tried to win the race; he'd just cruised over the line in tenth place, needing only the one point to claim an unassailable lead in the School Championship).

And so, with one race left in the Race School season, Jason had charged up in the Championship standings:

THE INTERNATIONAL RACE SCHOOL CHAMPIONSHIP STANDIINGS				
AFTER 49 RACES				
DRIVER		**NO.**	**CAR**	**POINTS**
1.	XONORA, X.	1	*Speed Razor*	307
2.	KRISHNA, V.	31	*Calcutta-IV*	296
3.	WASHINGTON, I.	42	*Black Bullet*	278
4.	BECKER, B.	09	*Devil's Chariot*	276
5.	CHASER, J.	55	*Argonaut*	276.
6.	PIPER, A.	16	*Pied Piper*	275
7.	WONG, H.	888	*Little Tokyo*	274.
8.	SCHUMACHER, K	25	*Blue Lightning*	273

Xavier was untouchable with 307 points, the Championship his.

Varishna Krishna, with 296 points, was also going to New York no matter what happened in Race 50.

But below them, it was a six-way tussle for the final two invitations to New York. Any one of the next six racers could—depending on the finishing order in Race 50—come in in the top four.

Jason and Barnaby Becker were level with 276 points each, tied at fourth in the standings (and now one point ahead of Ariel, whose niggling technical problems in recent races had hurt her badly).

But they weren't *truly* tied—if Barnaby and Jason ended the season with equal points (for example, they both crashed in Race 50), Barnaby would beat Jason on a countback, since he had come in second in Race 49 when Jason had come in third.

In the end, for Jason, there was only one option in Race 50: *He had to beat Barnaby Becker* and, if he finished low in the standings, he had to hope some other results went his way. But with Barnaby's new allies also out there on the track, just *finishing* Race 50 was going to be a tough prospect indeed.

• • •

To cap it all off, the final race of the year was the perfect kind of race to conclude the season.

Designed to test every hover car racing skill imaginable, it was to take place on the rarely used Course 13—a superdifficult track that began by stretching southward, down over the Southern Ocean along a superlong straight-away, before it transformed into a twisting, turning series of bends that weaved between the outer icebergs of Antarctica.

In that section of the course, racers could—if they were prepared to take the risk—opt to take one of three short-cuts between the bergs, but every shortcut ran between two bergs that clashed together (thanks to an underwater mechanism), giving them the name the "Clashing Bergs." The standard course did not run through any clashing bergs, but it was longer. High risk, high reward.

After that, the course turned back north, returning to Tasmania, where the racers had to slow dramatically to negotiate the tight highways of the island, before reaching the Finish Line in Hobart.

Each lap took about fourteen minutes. And since Race 50

was a fifty-one-lap enduro—that meant a twelve-hour race.

But there was one more feature of Race 50 that made it an absolute killer: Not only was it a test of endurance and skill, but it was also a test of race positioning—Race 50 was a Last-Man Drop-Off race.

Technically, it was classified as a "51-3-1" Super-Enduro Last-Man Drop-Off," meaning: It would be fifty-one laps, and every three laps, the last-placed racer would be eliminated, until only four racers remained to fight out a six-lap sprint to the finish, a sprint that would involve one last pit stop.

Which made Jason's battle with Barnaby even more perilous: If Jason was eliminated at any time *before* Barnaby, Barnaby would be going to New York.

After all that, perhaps only one thing was clear.

Race 50 would be run on a knife-edge: It would be a dogfight of hardcore racing, under the ever-present threat of last-man elimination.

Race 50 made no allowance for mistakes.

It would be winner take all.

Jason woke up with a start, gasping and sweating.

Another crash nightmare.

"What is wrong with me?" he whispered aloud.

He checked the digital clock beside his bed. It was 1:30 a.m. It was the middle of the night—the night before Race 50. Just what he needed.

He sat up and decided that sleep would be impossible, at least for a while.

He went for a walk, wandered down to a small enclosed garden overlooking the river, to gaze at the fountains there.

He sat down on a bench—and suddenly heard footsteps

on gravel and voices in the darkness. He ducked behind a statue, listened.

He could make out two voices. One old and deep, the other younger, slimier.

Older voice: "Good work. You've slowed her rise up in the Championship standings."

Younger voice: "Only doing what I'm told."

Older voice: "But she *can* still finish in the top four. And this school does not want to see Ms. Piper going to New York. It's been embarrassing enough having her study here for the year—and then that Chaser boy gave her a whole heap of publicity in Italy—but it would be beyond the pale if she ended up *representing* the school in New York. I need you to make sure she doesn't."

Younger voice: "After the Becker incident at the tournament, we can't deplete her magneto drives with microwaves anymore. Worms and viruses in her pit machine have worked recently, but she put in a new firewall two days ago and it's a good one. That said, I think I can find a newer virus that can bring her system down."

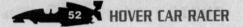

Older voice: "Make it happen."

There was a crunching of gravel and the two speakers were gone.

Jason's eyes were wide with shock.

He recognized both voices.

The older voice had belonged to Jean-Pierre LeClerq.

And the younger one: Wernold Smythe, the nasty grease monkey from the school's Parts and Equipment Department.

Jason returned to bed.

Before the race tomorrow, he'd have to have a word with Ariel.

Dawn came on the day of Race 50.

It found Jason sitting on a clifftop with Dido, the two of them gazing out at the ocean sunrise. Despite his sleepless night, they'd arranged to meet and, truth be told, Jason wanted to see Dido alone before the race—her presence gave him strength.

On the horizon, dark clouds framed the rising sun.

"So how are you feeling today?" Dido asked him.

"Better," he said firmly. "Stronger."

His eyes were fixed forward. Game face.

"And your plan for Barnaby?"

"Solid," he said. "We've found a chink in his technique.

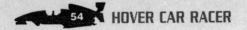

The Bug's been analyzing his racing maneuvers on videodisc. Barnaby's weak on right-hand hairpins—that's where he gets sloppy; he goes too wide, so you can cut inside him. And this track is tight. Lots of hairpins."

Dido grabbed his hand. "Good luck, Jason."

"Thanks."

Jason looked at the dark clouds on the horizon. "It's going to rain today."

Rain hammered down on the straightaway in front of the starting gates.

Sheltered from the driving rain, nineteen hover cars sat poised in their gates, their magneto drives thrumming, pilots and navigators hunched in their cockpits, ready. (Due to mechanical problems and other issues, six students were sitting out the race.)

The Race School's starting gates were based on those used in old Roman chariot races: A wide arc-shaped structure fitted with thirty archways opened onto the wide straightaway. Each archway housed one car, and at the starter's signal, steel grills barring them

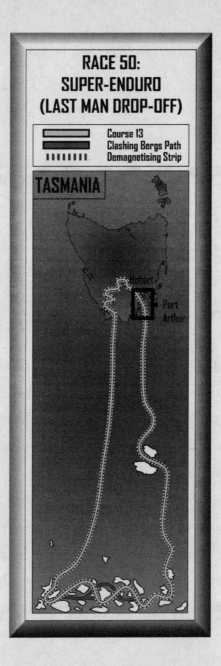

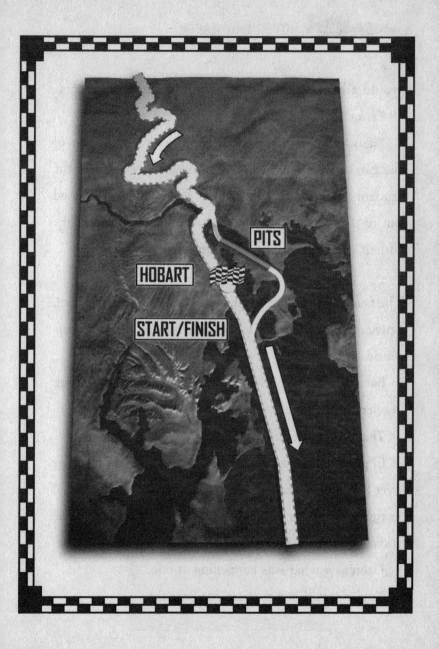

would all spring open together, unleashing the racers.

Clang!

The grills burst open, and, like horses leaping out of the gates in the Melbourne Cup, the nineteen cars of the students of the International Race School blasted out of their archways, into the rain, and commenced the fiftieth and final race of the Race School season.

The field shoomed due south out over the Southern Ocean, noses into the driving rain, heading for the bottom of the world.

Barnaby Becker immediately took the lead—with Xavier slotting in close behind him.

This was unusual.

In previous races, Xavier had shown a clear advantage over Barnaby in straight-line speed, yet now he just settled in tight behind his stablemate . . . as if he were glad to be traveling at three-quarter pace.

Jason saw what was happening at once.

Xavier was riding shotgun for Barnaby.

He was *protecting* his stablemate.

Not needing any points for himself, Xavier was trying to ensure that Barnaby won the race—thus getting Barnaby into the top four, and ensuring that Jason didn't go to New York.

But no sooner had he realized this than Jason faced another, more immediate problem.

For it was at that moment—as they swept low over the rain-battered waves of the Southern Ocean—that some of the other racers started targeting the *Argonaut*.

Joaquin Cortez zeroed in on Jason from the right, aiming *straight for* his tailfin!

The blow would have knocked them both out of the race, but Cortez—not in contention for a place in the top four—didn't seem to care at all. Jason ducked under him, swooping low, avoiding the blow—

—at which moment Horatio Wong rammed him from the other side, banging into the *Argonaut*'s left wing, before zooming ahead of Jason. Unlike Cortez, Wong still had a chance of making the top four, and he wasn't going to jeopardize that just yet.

"Jason!" Sally's voice came in. *"What the hell is happening!"*

"Cortez just tried a kamikaze run, tried to knock us out of the race!" Jason called. "Barnaby must have bought him!"

"What are you going to do?"

"There's only one thing we can do, outrun him."

Jason gunned the accelerator as they hit the pair of icebergs halfway down the Southern Ocean straightaway—known as the Chicane—and leaped ahead of Cortez, now in seventh place behind Barnaby (1), Xavier (2), Varishna Krishna (3), Isaiah Washington (4), Ariel (5), and Wong (6); but with Joaquin Cortez nipping at his heels, trying to find an opportunity to take him out.

Then it was into the iceberg section.

If he could have, Jason would have gaped at the spectacle of the field of mammoth bergs, but there was no time for gawking now. He banked the *Argonaut* between the white monoliths, following the path of the demag lights.

Between the white monoliths

At this early stage in the race, everyone took the standard route between the icebergs.

But as Jason well knew, as the race went on and things got desperate, that would change.

After three laps, the eliminations began.

At first, they were relatively unobtrusive. Minor racers crashed in the tight, land-bound sections of the course, or racers succumbed to technical mishaps—thus eliminating themselves.

Barnaby continued to lead, with Xavier shadowing him in second place.

Then came Krishna, Washington, Ariel, and Wong.

Followed by Jason and Cortez.

But then, as the number of racers diminished, things really did start to get desperate.

RACE 50

LAP: 35 OF 51

RACERS LEFT ON TRACK: 8

By Lap 35, Jason was still in seventh place—second to last.

He was starting to worry.

The main thing he had to do in this race was beat Barnaby and, at the moment, Barnaby was way out in first place, protected by Xavier, while Jason was still way back in seventh—with a total of eight racers still on the track and five of them between him and Barnaby.

Jason still had Horatio Wong directly in front of him in sixth and Joaquin Cortez behind him in eighth.

Cortez continued to badger Jason, especially in the

iceberg section of the track, trying to axe through the *Argonaut*'s tailfin by taking the turns straighter than Jason—recklessly straighter.

In the end, it was Cortez's determination to nail Jason that was his undoing. At one point amid the icebergs, Jason took one turn a little too wide, offering Cortez a clear straight-line charge at his exposed tailfin. Cortez took the opportunity, not realizing that it wasn't an opportunity at all—it was bait.

Because suddenly Jason banked the other way, leaving Cortez to smash hard into the side of an iceberg.

Ejection. Explosion.

Cortez's car was history, and the Mexican racer and his navigator soon found themselves floating down to earth on hover chutes. And as Jason completed Lap 36 several minutes later, Cortez was eliminated.

But now Jason was in last place—with Horatio Wong banking and bending in front of him.

Jason had three laps to overtake Wong.

Lap 37—no dice. Wong fended him off grimly, at times using dubious defensive tactics.

Lap 38—Jason flew the entire lap within a yard of Wong's tail, but no matter what he tried, he *still* couldn't pass Wong.

Jason began to panic. He was running out of time and track.

He zoomed through Hobart again, and started Lap 39, knowing it could well be his last.

And as he rocketed down the long Southern Ocean straightaway, eyeing Wong's weaving taillights, he made the call.

"Bug," he said. "Either we get past this jerk on this lap or we're out! Out of the race, out of contention to go to New York, out of everything. I say we take him via the Clashing Bergs. Opinions?"

The Bug replied instantly . . . and firmly.

"I'll take that as a yes," Jason said.

The leaders rushed into the iceberg section of the course, all taking the standard route, Wong among them.

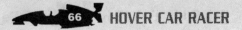

But as Wong swept right, taking the regulation route, Jason abruptly cut left, slicing between some smaller icebergs before he beheld two clashing bergs.

They were absolutely gigantic.

The rough seas of the ocean and the underwater mechanism caused the two big icebergs to alternately slide apart and then clang back together like a pair of god-size cymbals. The enormous bulk of the two bergs—each was easily 330 feet long—meant that a racer had to really floor it in order to get through.

Jason floored it.

The *Argonaut* screamed into the shadowy canyon between the two bergs just as they reached their widest point.

Then the two bergs converged.

The *Argonaut* sped—

The canyon narrowed, its towering white walls closing—

The Bug screamed—

And Jason flipped the *Argonaut* onto its side as the

canyon's walls became unbearably close and—
CRASH!—the two icebergs came together with a deafening boom *just as* the tiny *Argonaut* blasted out from
between them, house-size chunks of ice raining down into
the water behind it.

"*Hoo-ah!*" Jason yelled, blood pulsing through his
veins as he swooped back onto the track proper . . . three
car-lengths ahead of Wong!

In sixth place.

Wong's eyes went wide. He couldn't believe it—Jason
was now in front of him!

"Okay . . . ," Jason said, his eyes now laser-focused.
"Time to put you *out*, Horatio."

And put him out, he did.

No matter what Wong threw at him, Jason fended him
off, and as Lap 39 ended, it was Wong who found himself
in seventh place, last place.

And out of the race.

RACE 50

LAP: 40 OF 51

RACERS LEFT ON TRACK: 6

So by Lap 40, the race order was this:

    1: Barnaby.

    2: Xavier.

    3: Krishna.

    4: Ariel.

    5: Isaiah Washington.

    6: Jason.

As one would expect of such an important race, it was superclose—while he was in last place, Jason was still flying within sight of the leaders.

Then, at the end of Lap 41, everyone pitted.

• • •

Jason swung into the pits, to see all the other pit bays teeming with activity. In a race as long as this one, pit stops were longer, taking anywhere between thirty and fifty seconds.

As he arrived, he saw Barnaby shoom back out onto the track—closely followed by Krishna and Ariel, but not, surprisingly, by Xavier Xonora. For some reason, Xavier was still in his pit bay.

Jason came to his own bay.

Sally immediately went to work, and outdid herself.

She performed a superb stop, so superb that Jason came out of his pit bay before Isaiah Washington did, leapfrogging him into fifth place.

He gunned the *Argonaut* out of its pit bay—

—only to slam on the brakes a moment later.

A car was blocking the exit tunnel that led back out to the track.

Xavier Xonora's *Speed Razor*.

It was just splayed across the tunnel, completely blocking the exit—as if it had stalled in the process of leaving

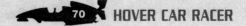

its own pit bay. Xavier offered Jason a disingenuous shrug: *Sorry. But it's not my fault.*

Seconds ticked by.

Jason fumed. "That skunk is blocking us!" He couldn't believe it. Every second he was held up here by Xavier, Barnaby was racing away to victory.

And then Isaiah Washington appeared in Jason's rear-view mirrors, looming up behind the *Argonaut*. Only Washington didn't appear to be slowing. At this rate, *he was going to ram Jason's tailfin—*

To evade him, Jason started edging around Xavier's car. But then, just as he was about to get around Xavier, surprise-surprise, Xavier got the *Speed Razor* started and darted off ahead of Jason.

Jason could only swear and chase after him, still in fifth place ahead of Washington, but now a *long* way behind Barnaby Becker.

Jason raced hard through the rain.

He was now second to last and so safe from immediate

elimination, but directly in front of him was the tailfin of the all-black *Speed Razor*. And Jason had a feeling that Xavier wasn't going to let him past lightly.

At the end of the next lap, Lap 42, Isaiah Washington bowed out.

Five racers left.

Nine laps remaining.

One elimination to go before the six-lap dash to the Finish Line.

The race order was:

1: Barnaby Becker.

2: Varishna Krishna.

3: Ariel Piper.

4: Xavier.

5: Jason.

And suddenly Jason was again in last place—only now his situation was especially dire: Barnaby was way out in front, and the racer directly in front of Jason was Xavier, Barnaby's teammate.

Thus they began Lap 43 and, with a gulp, Jason saw

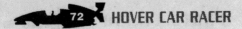

what he had to do: He had exactly three laps to get past the best racer at Race School—perhaps the best racer to have *ever* come to Race School—or else he'd be eliminated.

The *Speed Razor* and the *Argonaut*.

Going at it tooth and nail.

Jason threw everything he had at the Black Prince, but, try as he might, he just couldn't get past the *Speed Razor*.

Xavier was simply too good.

He just wouldn't let Jason by.

On Lap 43, Jason even tried another daring dash through the first pair of Clashing Bergs—just as he had done with Wong—but to his total horror, Xavier outran him by going *around* on the standard route!

That's impossible! Jason thought. *If he can outrun me*

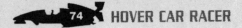

going around the Clashing Bergs, there's no way I can take him. . . .

For the rest of that lap, Xavier held him off easily, anticipating every one of Jason's overtaking maneuvers through the tight land-bound section of the course.

Lap 44: Still no luck. Xavier seemed to be enjoying this, blocking Jason, ruining his chances of beating Barnaby.

And then they hit Lap 45.

Jason's last chance.

The *Speed Razor* and the *Argonaut* shot down the Southern Ocean straightaway, zigzagged through the Chicane—and suddenly the Bug made a suggestion.

"You've got to be kidding . . . ," Sally said over the radio.

The Bug said he wasn't kidding.

"That's totally crazy, Bug! Even by your standards!" Sally said. *"You'll be killed for sure!"*

But Jason liked the plan. "Nice thinking, Bug. You always were a daredevil at heart. Hang on to your hat, little brother, because this is gonna get hairy. . . ."

They came to the iceberg section—

And true to form, Xavier kept to the standard track—

While Jason took the Clashing Bergs track—

And, as before, Xavier beat them to the other side, even though he'd stayed on the regulation track. But Jason had gained a whole car-length on him.

Then they came to the second fork in the track—leading to the second set of Clashing Bergs—and again Xavier took the safe option, but not Jason.

To everyone's surprise, including Xavier's, he took the Clashing Bergs track *again*—

And this time, he came out the other end *alongside Xavier*—

They hit the third and last fork together . . . and *again* Jason took the Clashing Bergs option!

Xavier went the long way—

Jason shot through a quickly narrowing chasm of two gargantuan icebergs—

—and blasted out the other end just as they clashed, only this time when he emerged, he came out exactly one car-length *ahead* of Xavier!

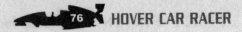

It had taken not one, not two, but three shortcuts to do the impossible: They had overtaken Xavier!

Xavier charged, threw all he had at Jason, trying to retake him. But now that he was in front, Jason wasn't going to let go of his lead.

He and Xavier fought all the way around the track, but when they hit the Finish Line seven minutes later, it was Jason in the lead.

The fifteenth and last elimination of the race would be Xavier Xonora.

Now there were only four racers left, and with six laps to go, they alone would fight it out to the finish.

But not before one last pit stop at the end of Lap 48.

Jason knew this pit stop would be his last chance to catch up to Barnaby—who by this time was almost 40 seconds ahead of him.

"Sally!" he called over the radio. "This is your moment!"

"I'll be waiting," came the reply.

Jason wound through the land-bound section of the course, until finally he beheld Hobart.

He swept into the city and dived into the pits—

—saw the usual buzz of activity, mech chiefs running every which way, pit machines rising and falling, electric lights everywhere blazing.

He saw the other three racers still in their pit bays, their mech chiefs working away already, halfway through their stops:

Barnaby.

Krishna.

Ariel.

And then, just as Jason swung the *Argonaut* into its pit bay, there came a loud dying whine from somewhere above him and all of a sudden . . .

. . . *every single electric light* in Pit Lane went out!

Pit machines froze in midair.

Computer monitors crashed to black.

Everyone looked about themselves in confusion.

Sally, now standing beside the *Argonaut*, swapped a look with Jason.

They didn't even need to say it out loud.

Power failure.

Manual pit stop.

Jason and the Bug were out of their seats in seconds, and by hand they attached six fresh magneto drives to the *Argonaut* while Sally added coolant and compressed-air cylinders, also by hand.

The other teams obviously hadn't practiced manual stops much—if at all—and they just stood in their pit bays, confused.

Barnaby yelled at his mech chief, swearing, pointing, telling him to hurry up.

Krishna deduced that he had to help his mech chief, and so he leaped out of his car.

Ariel did the same—and while she may not have practiced manual stops as well as Jason's team, of the other three racers, she did the best at it.

As he screwed on his mag drives with a cordless drill, Jason heard Ariel's mech chief yell to Ariel: "—can't explain it! Some kind of virus just hit us like a goddarn anvil! Ripped down our firewall! But it was so powerful, it spread into the wider system and brought down the entire Pit Lane power grid!'

In the end, the big winners from the unexpected power shutdown were Ariel and Jason.

Having entered the pits in third place, Ariel shot back out onto the track in first place!

Krishna shot out next, in second.

Barnaby was the biggest loser—perhaps because he hadn't gotten out of his car during the entire manual stop, choosing instead to simply abuse his mech chief. As such, he came out of the pits in third place . . .

. . . a single car-length ahead of Jason Chaser.

Game on.

RACE 50

LAP: 50 OF 51

RACERS LEFT ON TRACK: 4

With two laps to go, Jason hammered at the heels of Barnaby Becker.

In a funny way, Jason felt confident now.

Xavier was out of the race, as were those racers like Cortez and Wong who had tried to take him out. And now he had Barnaby in his sights.

And he knew Barnaby's weakness—right-hand hairpins—and there were plenty of those coming up.

Through the Chicane . . . into the icebergs.

Jason lined up Barnaby.

Got himself into position behind him.

The best option was at the very end of the iceberg section, at a hairpin turn inside a tunnel carved into the last iceberg.

They weaved through the icebergs, Jason coming closer and closer to Barnaby—looming ominously.

Then they hit the last iceberg, and Jason made his move, ducked inside Barnaby, expecting him to take it wide, as usual . . .

. . . only Barnaby didn't do that at all.

Instead he took the hairpin perfectly and cut Jason off . . .

. . . and held his position!

Jason was shocked.

That wasn't supposed to happen! his mind screamed.

Barnaby never took hairpins like that—not even in the most recent race, Race 49.

He must've gotten lucky, Jason thought, and he prepared to take Barnaby at a right-hand hairpin up in the land-bound section of the track.

But again Barnaby confounded him—taking that

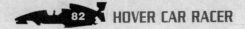

hairpin perfectly as well, and thus fending Jason off again.

"How are you doing this, Barnaby!" Jason asked aloud. "How do you know . . . ?"

He cut himself off.

At that moment, like a sledgehammer blow, it hit him . . .

. . . and it broke his heart.

Dido.

Flashback:

Jason and Dido that morning, sitting on the clifftop watching the sunrise. And Jason telling Dido how he planned to beat Barnaby that day:

"We've found a chink in his technique. The Bug's been analyzing his racing maneuvers on videodisc. Barnaby's weak on right-hand hairpins—that's where he gets sloppy; he goes too wide, so you can cut inside him. . . ."

Then another recollection struck Jason.

The time he had told Dido about his nightmares and his greatest fear: having his tailfin taken out. Then, the very next day, Horatio Wong had ruthlessly taken out his tailfin, almost killing him and the Bug.

His greatest fear at the time had come true.

And the event had all but taken Jason over the edge, shattering his race confidence.

Oh, Dido . . ., he thought. *You didn't . . .*

But the evidence was clear. Whenever he told Dido something, his enemies seemed to know it the following day.

Dido was in league with Barnaby and Xavier.

Jason's brain returned to Race 50.

The *Argonaut* screamed across the Finish Line and started the last lap, Lap 51.

Ariel was leading.

Krishna was in second place.

Then a gap.

Then Barnaby in third.

And Jason in fourth.

Race 50 had essentially become two races: one between

Ariel and Krishna for the win and another between Barnaby and Jason for third place.

But as far as Jason was concerned, Krishna and Ariel didn't matter—however they finished, it didn't affect him in the overall standings. All he had to do was beat Barnaby to get to New York: As things were, third was as good as first in this race.

Down the Southern Ocean straightaway, through the Chicane for the last time.

He was still all over Barnaby, probing for a way past.

Into the iceberg section.

Jason thought about taking the three Clashing Bergs routes again, but figured his luck there couldn't last. Better to hang on to Barnaby's tail—he could still take him.

But he couldn't pass him in the icebergs.

Barnaby held him out, sometimes just by flagrantly taking up all the track, blocking Jason's path.

Northward, back toward Tasmania.

Then into the land-bound section.

More hairpins, and belying his previous efforts, Barnaby took them all beautifully—but now Jason was charging, pushing Barnaby on every turn, the two cars almost side by side.

As Jason and Barnaby fought in the central region of Tasmania, ahead of them, Ariel Piper—having flown a near-perfect race—crossed the Finish Line five seconds ahead of Varishna Krishna, taking first place.

But Barnaby and Jason were still racing.

And with Ariel and Krishna coming in first and second, everything was still on the line for the two of them—whoever won this tussle would go to New York.

Screaming with speed, they came roaring over the magnificent Tasman Bridge, approaching the last corner of the race—a sharp *left*-hand hairpin underneath a freeway flyover—and Jason made a sudden inside move on the turn . . .

. . . and he got him!

As the Finish Line swept into view, the *Argonaut*'s

nose inched in front of the nose of the *Devil's Chariot*.

"Noooo!" Barnaby yelled.

And then he did something totally unexpected.

Panicked and desperate, Barnaby rammed Jason hard—driving *both* of their cars across the nearest set of demag lights.

Jason fought with his steering wheel, but to no avail— he saw his mag levels deplete with shocking speed.

Luckily for him, the same thing was happening to Barnaby's car. It, too, was losing all its magnetic power.

At which point Jason saw where he was heading— straight for a big concrete pylon that supported the freeway bridge above them.

With a terrible shriek, the *Argonaut* glanced off the pylon and flipped up onto its side, ending three-quarters sideways, lying up against the next concrete pylon.

The *Devil's Chariot* performed a similar crash, but it finished right side up, resting on the roadway, pointing backward.

Both cars just sat there, under the concrete overpass, smoking and still.

"You okay?" Jason yelled to the Bug, both of them hanging sideways in their seatbelts.

The Bug said he was.

Jason was all right too, but the forward half of the *Argonaut* was now resting on its side up against the pylon, so Jason couldn't get out of the cockpit even if he tried.

"Bug! Pro rules! Driver over the Line. You've got to get to the Finish Line! Here!"

Jason removed the *Argonaut*'s steering wheel—fitted as it was with a transponder. Pro rules dictated that if a car couldn't cross the line, a racer could still finish the race by having either himself or his navigator *carry* his transponder-equipped steering wheel over the line.

Jason offered the steering wheel to the Bug. "Run! *Run!*"

The Bug's eyes boggled for a moment, then he unbuckled his seatbelt and literally fell out of the cockpit, dropping

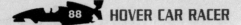

clumsily to the ground. Then he stood up, took the steering wheel from Jason, and ran.

Down the highway.

As fast as his little legs could carry him, down the last 1,600 feet of the track.

The crowd gathered to watch the final race of the season had never seen anything like it.

There was the Bug, *running* down the finishing straight-away, his little legs pumping, his round bespectacled face pink with exertion, clutching a steering wheel in his right fist.

Trapped in the cockpit of the *Argonaut*, Jason could only watch him run.

"Go, Bug! Go!"

Vmmmmmm.

Just then, an ominous thrumming sound came to life beside Jason.

Jason turned—to see the battered and dented *Devil's Chariot* lift up off the asphalt and resume a hovering position. It seemed wounded, broken. But it was working.

Slowly, it pivoted in midair and Jason saw Barnaby at the controls, his face set in an evil grimace.

Jason snapped around—and saw the Bug still running down the road.

Barnaby hit the gas.

The Bug ran. Hard.

He was hardly built for speed: short legs, little pot belly, big glasses, helmet. Sweat had fogged up his glasses by now, but he kept on pounding the pavement anyway.

The crowd was now on its feet—but silent. Stunned into silence.

And then everyone saw it.

Saw Barnaby Becker's battered *Devil's Chariot* come lurching down the highway behind the Bug . . .

Chasing him to the end.

It wasn't trying to run him down. Far from it. It was

trying to beat him to the line. After all the racing, all the pit stops and passing maneuvers, it had come down to this: one racer on foot, the other in the air, in his dented, broken car.

And as all could see, even at their wildly differing speeds, they would hit the line almost together. . . .

Then, a man's voice in the crowd yelled, "Go, Bug! Go!"

The voice of Henry Chaser.

And as they watched this bizarre contest, the rest of the crowd joined in.

"GO, BUG! GO!"

"GO, BUG! GO!"

The Bug's little legs pumped up and down.

The *Devil's Chariot* gained speed.

Jason could only watch, helpless in his seat.

The Bug ran over the giant white letters painted on the road just before the Finish Line—START-FINISH—just as the *Devil's Chariot* roared up behind him, accelerating . . .

. . . coming closer and closer and closer . . .

. . . and the Bug saw the line—the actual Finish Line, a thick white band stretching across the road in front of him—and as the roar of the *Devil's Chariot* filled his ears and rushed alongside him, he dived . . .

RACE 50

LAP: 51 OF 51

RACERS LEFT ON TRACK: 4

It would go down in Race School history as one of the most bizarre photo-finish snapshots ever.

It depicted the Bug, frozen in midair, *diving* over the Finish Line, the *Argonaut*'s steering wheel held in front of him in his outstretched hands—while the *Devil's Chariot* hovered, also frozen, in the background of the photo, its body blurred with speed . . . and its nose a bare four inches *short of* the line.

Thanks to the Bug's little legs, Team *Argonaut* had beaten Barnaby Becker by less than a foot.

Bizarre photo finish

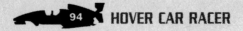

Afterward, Henry Chaser would ask if he could have a copy of the photo, and the school would give him one.

It now hangs in the Chaser family living room.

Pandemonium reigned in the pits after the results of Race 50 became apparent.

Jason leaped out of the recently towed-in *Argonaut* and threw his fists into the air. Sally caught him, also jumping for joy.

They knew the score.

The results of Race 50 had changed the Race School Championship standings dramatically.

It now looked like this:

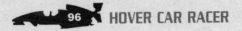

	THE INTERNATIONAL RACE SCHOOL CHAMPIONSHIP STANDINGS AFTER 50 RACES			
	DRIVER	**NO.**	**CAR**	**POINTS**
1.	XONORA, X.	1	*Speed Razor*	313
2.	KRISHNA, V.	31	*Calcutta-IV*	305
3.	PIPER, A.	16	*Pied Piper*	285
4.	CHASER, J.	55	*Argonaut*	284
5.	BECKER, B.	09	*Devil's Chariot*	283
6.	WASHINGTON, I.	42	*Black Bullet*	283
7.	WONG, H.	888	*Little Tokyo*	278
8.	SCHUMACHER, K.	25	*Blue Lightning*	275

Suddenly the top four looked very different.

Barnaby and Isaiah Washington had both dropped out of it completely, replaced by Ariel—who with her ten-point win had leaped up from sixth to third—and Jason, who had gone from fifth to fourth with his eight points for coming in third.

Along with Xavier and Krishna, Jason and Ariel were going to New York.

Almost as pleasing to Jason was the result that Barnaby Becker and Isaiah Washington wouldn't be going anywhere.

But then something else happened—ripping Jason from his thoughts.

Dido ran into the pits.

She spotted Jason, smiled with joy, and hurried over to the *Argonaut*.

Dido threw her arms around Jason . . .

. . . but Jason didn't hug her back.

She noticed his lack of response immediately and drew away. "What's wrong, Jason? You did it. You made the top four. You won your ticket to the New York Challenger Race."

At first, Jason didn't speak. Truth be told, he actually didn't know what to say. He'd never had someone so brazenly betray his trust before.

For a long moment, he just looked at Dido—scanned her eyes, her face, searching for something . . . anything.

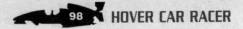

Something he could trust, something he could believe in.

But he found nothing there.

Both the Bug and Sally saw at once that something was very wrong—but they kept their distance.

"Jason? Are you okay?" Dido asked.

"I have something to tell you," Jason said. "Something very personal . . ."

"Yes," Dido said gently.

"So I hope when you relay it to Xavier and Barnaby, you tell it to them word for word."

The blood drained from Dido's face.

The Bug spun in disbelief. Sally McDuff turned too.

Dido stammered, "Jason . . . I . . . what are you say—"

"I know what you did, Dido," Jason said. "You were feeding them everything I told you. About my fears. About my strategies, like overtaking Barnaby on hairpins. Stuff I never told anyone else. You were probably also updating them about my health. I'm also now wondering about some of those late nights we had before important races—like in Italy. I'm wondering if you were *keeping* me out late."

Dido fell silent.

By now Sally was staring daggers at her. The Bug's mouth was just open in shock.

Jason went on. "Even that time in the coffee shop, when Barnaby hit on you and you blew him off, I bet that was a setup, too."

As if in reply, Dido bowed her head.

"So when you see them next time," Jason said, "tell them this from me: *Jason Chaser is back. Back to full strength.* Which means the next time we're all on the same track, they're going *down.* As for you, Dido, please leave."

Dido clutched her face, then turned and ran away.

Steely eyed, Jason could only watch her go.

In the immediate aftermath of Race 50, questions were asked about the catastrophic power failure that had occurred during the final pit stop on Lap 48.

Race Director Calder led the investigations . . .

. . . and quickly made some sensational findings.

Ariel's mech chief had been right: On Lap 48, Ariel's pit machine had indeed been hit by a superpowerful computer virus.

But only that morning, Ariel—tipped off by Jason before the race—had installed a new firewall on her system and it had repelled the sinister virus. Unfortunately the virus then searched for a new host and it found it in the school's power grid.

And so, like a constricting python, the virus wrapped itself around the school's power system . . . and brought down the entire grid!

The source computer for the virus was soon found: Wernold Smythe's computer in the Parts and Equipment Department.

Smythe was confronted and he broke down in seconds, implicating no less than the principal of the school, Jean-Pierre LeClerq, in a plot to damage Ariel Piper's chances at the Race School, a plot that went all the way back to her depleted mags in Race 1. And why?

Because she was a girl.

LeClerq protested his innocence, but the look on his face said it all. He'd done it, all right.

The school's board held an emergency meeting that night and suspended LeClerq, pending further investigation. In the meantime, Race Director Calder—a man of impeccable integrity—would be acting principal in his place.

Ariel and Jason just watched the drama unfold from afar.

"Thanks for the tipoff this morning," Ariel said as they watched LeClerq skulk away from the Race School, get into his car, and drive off in a huff.

"Anytime," Jason said. "Anytime."

The following evening, the school held its annual end-of-year Presentation Dinner.

It was a formal affair, with parents, friends, and some sponsors in attendance, and hosted by Acting Principal Calder.

Jason sat at a table with Team *Argonaut*, plus his parents and—for the first time that year—Sally's entire family, including her parents and all eight of her very proud racing-mad brothers, newly arrived from Scotland.

As he sat down, Jason noticed Dido over at Xavier Xonora's table, sitting alongside Xavier.

"I asked around," Sally whispered to Jason, seeing him

looking at Dido. "She's Xavier's cousin. But she's not royalty. Her mom is the queen of Monesi's sister; lives in Italy."

"We met in Italy," Jason said. "Just before the Italian Run. I thought it was luck, coincidence, fate. But it wasn't. It was a setup, a big setup, and I fell for it.'

Sally tousled his hair. "Jason, if it makes you feel any better, if Xavier had sent a gorgeous young Italian studmuffin to seduce me for our race secrets, I woulda told him everything too."

"Really?"

"Oh, sure," she said, "but not before I *smooched the living daylights* out of the young stallion!"

She roared with laughter, clapped Jason on the back. "Now, shut up, eat, and enjoy yourself, you big superstar."

After the main course had been served, the usual prizes were handed out.

It was virtually a clean sweep for the *Speed Razor*.

First-place driver in the Championship standings: Xavier. For that he took home a huge trophy.

The Race School medal for the year's best driver also went to Xavier.

The teachers' choice of Best Mech Chief was Xavier's crew chief, Oliver Koch—although his victory was narrow: He only beat out Sally McDuff by two votes.

Jason didn't win a single prize.

But then he didn't actually mind that.

He'd had an incredible year at Race School, but for him, Race School wasn't about winning prizes, it was about scoring a contract with a pro team—and he'd already had one run with a pro team in Italy this year.

And if he—just maybe—won the New York Challenger Race, he might race again in a pro event: The winner of the Challenger got an automatic "exemption invitation" to participate in the Masters.

That said, there was one prize handed out that evening which Jason felt he had played some part in.

For one prize eluded Xavier's table—the prize for Teacher of the Year. It was a peculiar omission, as many would have credited Xavier's winning efforts to Zoroastro's superior instruction.

But then, not a few officials at the Race School still recalled Barnaby Becker's disgraceful acts during the Sponsors' Tournament—and they secretly thought Zoroastro had played a part in that.

Which was why the prize for Teacher of the Year went to Scott Syracuse.

Last of all, and rather fittingly, the night ended with the four racers who would represent the Race School at the New York Challenger Race—Xavier, Krishna, Ariel, and Jason—called to the stage to receive a standing ovation from their family and friends.

A week later, Jason found himself sitting once again on a grassy headland, watching the sun rising over the ocean. With him were Sally and the Bug, also gazing at the dawn.

Suddenly—*vroom!*—a police hover copter roared by overhead, invading the view.

It flew away to the left, out toward the spectacular sky-line of New York City.

Jason eyed the dense collection of towering sky-scrapers, swooping suspension bridges, and countless lights of Manhattan Island.

And his eyes narrowed.

PART II

CHALLENGER

NEW YORK CITY, USA

New York City, glorious in the fall.

Rust-colored leaves littered Central Park. The Chrysler Building glittered like a diamond. The Brooklyn Bridge floated high on its new hover pylons. And the Twin Pillars of Light—the pair of light shafts that rose from the spot where the Twin Towers had once stood—soared into the sky.

And with the fall, came the race teams.

Because in the fall, for one week, the largest city in America was transformed into a series of the most incredible street circuits in racing.

Fifth Avenue became Race HQ, with the Start-Finish

Line set up outside the main entrance to the Empire State Building. Supersteep multilevel hover stands lined the broad boulevard.

The pits were situated on Sixth Avenue, parallel to Fifth—racers reached them by branching off Fifth Avenue at the New York Public Library and running southward behind the Empire State Building.

Filling the air above the avenues and streets of New York City was a phenomenon peculiar to Masters Week: *confetti snow*.

It filled the concrete canyons of the city—a beautiful, slow-falling rain of white paper. In celebration of their racing carnival, New Yorkers hurled tiny pieces of shredded paper out their windows, creating a constant—and stunning—mist of white confetti that floated down into their streets. The roads themselves had to be cleaned each evening, since by the end of a given day they would be three inches deep in the stuff.

Today was Monday—a general preparation day.

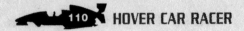

Tuesday would see the running of the Challenger Race—widely regarded as a showpiece for the world's up-and-coming drivers.

Wednesday was Parade Day—when all of the sixteen racers who had qualified for the Masters would travel down Fifth Avenue before the adoring crowds.

Then on Thursday it would all start, one race per day over four sensational days, with the number of racers reduced by four every day. It was kind of like a Last Man Drop-Off, *but over the whole series of races*—after each race, the last four racers on the scoreboard were eliminated—until only four racers took part in the fourth and final race.

On Thursday, **Race 1: The Liberty Supersprint**—a tight-lap race through the streets of New York, with a short section of track that whipped out and around the Statue of Liberty. It was here that the racers had to negotiate the sharpest turn in the racing world, a 9-G hairpin corner known as Liberty's Elbow. It was not unknown for racers to black out on this notorious bend.

Friday, **Race 2: The Manhattan Gate Race**—250 gates set amid the labyrinthine grid of New York streets.

Saturday, **Race 3: The Pursuit**—a collective pursuit race in which the drivers raced in circuits around Manhattan Island. Its main feature: bridge-mounted ion waterfalls— glorious but deadly curtains of ionized particles that fell from each of Manhattan's many bridges; the waterfalls nullified *all* magnetic power in any hover car that strayed through them. The final turn of every lap of this race was Liberty's Elbow; the Finish Line: the Brooklyn Bridge.

And then, on Sunday, came the final race of the series, **Race 4: The Quest.** The longest race of the Masters, it took racers away from Manhattan Island, up the rural highways of New York State and through the great underground water-caverns to Niagara Falls on the Canadian border. There, each racer had to grab their "trophy"—an item they had sent there earlier in the morning—and then bring it back to New York City. The first racer across the line with their trophy won.

Jason loved it. Every year, he would sit at home and,

with his dad beside him, watch every minute of the Masters Series on TV over the course of the whole week.

He'd always dreamed of coming to New York to watch the Masters in person, but it was a long way and tickets were terribly expensive and his family had never been able to afford it. The closest he'd come to seeing it was staying with his cousins in New Jersey and watching some of the races from a distance.

But now, now he was here, in New York (albeit staying with those same cousins in New Jersey), racing in the Challenger Race—with an outside chance of participating in the Masters.

Hell, he thought, even if he bombed out of the Challenger, he'd hang around for the Masters festival just for the chance to watch it up close.

This, for Jason, was *fantastic*.

This was a dream come true.

THE CHALLENGER RACE (TUESDAY)
15 MINS TO RACE START

The start gates stretched across Fifth Avenue. Like school races, the Challenger Race didn't have a pole position shootout. It gave everyone an equal start.

Cars entered their gates from behind, getting ready to race.

Jason eyed the other racers—the best from their respective leagues, regions, and schools.

Markos Christos—from Greece, in his car, the *Arion*, numbered 12 in honor of the twelve labors of Hercules. Christos was the top-ranked driver in the European Satellite League, a subdivision of the International Pro Circuit.

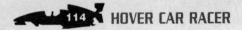

Eduardo—from the Central & South American Race School in Brazil. Like Xavier, he had won his School Championship, and from that, a pro contract with the low-level Castoldi Team. Since the CSA Race School wasn't as highly regarded as the International Race School, it had only been given two invitations to the Challenger Race.

Praveen Chandra, from the intense Indian Race School.

Zhang Lao, the third-placed driver from the Russo-Chinese League—a gun pilot from the Chinese Air Force. His fighter-shaped car, the *Chun-T'I*, was numbered 8, since the Chinese believe eight to be the luckiest number of all.

And, most fearsome of all, the two top-ranked drivers from the Russo-Chinese League: the Russian twins, Igor and Vladimir Krotsky. In their sleek, identical Mig-90s, the *Red Devil I* and *Red Devil II*, Igor and Vlad had been responsible for no less than sixteen crashes in their league races, none of which had injured them, and one of which had been fatal. But then the Russo-Chinese League was known for its rough racing.

But the name on everyone's lips was Xavier Xonora.

He was the hot favorite to win with the bookmakers—his exceptional fourth-place finish in the Italian Run had made a huge impact. And word had spread of his dominance at the International Race School.

In total, there were thirty racers in the Challenger Race—talented young drivers from all over the globe, every single one of them knowing that victory here could change their lives.

Standing behind the line of start gates, Jason was just stepping into the *Argonaut* when someone arrived at his car.

Xavier. Dressed in his black race suit and holding his helmet.

And standing with him—just for psychological effect, Jason figured—was Dido.

"Just thought I would swing by and share with you an interesting statistic I've only just discovered, Mr. Chaser," Xavier said.

And standing with him was Dido.

"And what's that?"

Xavier smiled meanly. "Only on one occasion, when we've both raced, have you actually *won the race*. And that was way back in Race 25. And today, there's no prize for second place. Only the winner gets the exemption invitation to the Masters Series. And based on the statistics, when we race, *I don't often come second*." Xavier turned to go. "Just thought you should know."

"Thanks," Jason said. "I'll keep that in mind."

In truth, Jason had been thinking a lot about Xavier.

He knew full well his head-to-head record against the Black Prince: with the exception of Races 25 and 50 (and Xavier's lazy effort in Race 49, which didn't count), whenever they'd raced, Xavier had beaten him.

The simple fact of the matter was that Jason just couldn't overtake Xavier.

It had only been an outrageous move in Race 50—whipping through all three sets of Clashing Bergs—that had gotten him past Xavier then.

And so, this past week, Jason and his team had been working on strategies to get by the *Speed Razor*.

They'd watched the videodiscs of all the televised races Xavier had been in, both at Race School and outside it. They'd analyzed his pit stops and how his pit crew behaved during races.

And their conclusion: Xavier was the perfect racer. His defensive techniques were impenetrable, and his crew work all but flawless. Indeed, his mech chief, Oliver Koch, was so good, not only did he provide lightning-fast stops, he also kept Xavier appraised—on every lap—as to how far he was ahead of his rivals, and whether he was extending his lead, or whether they were gaining on him.

It was the total package.

"He's too good," Sally had said as they'd sat in front of the television the night before, watching Xavier's finish in the Italian Run: the *Speed Razor* whipped across the Finish Line, Xavier punching a fist into the air. "I can't find a single chink in his armor."

The Bug said something as well.

"*Nobody's* perfect, Bug," Jason said, staring closely at the TV. "Hey. Sally. Can you bring me the videodisc of the Sponsors' Tournament?"

Sally brought the disc, and they watched it. Watched Xavier cross the Finish Line ahead of his opponents, including Jason in the final. Every time he crossed the line, Xavier did the same thing: He punched his fist into the air.

Sally shrugged. "I think the pattern's pretty clear, Jason. Xavier races. Xavier wins."

"Yes, it is," Jason said quietly. Then abruptly his eyes lit up. "Sally. Race 25. The race where I beat him. Is there any tape of that one?"

"No," Sally said. "It wasn't recorded."

"But it *was* a photo finish. Do we have a copy of the photo?"

Sally shrugged. "Sure. I have it here somewhere." She grabbed her race file and pulled a photo from it, handed it to Jason.

Jason examined the photo closely.

And he smiled.

Both Sally and the Bug saw his lips curl upward.

"What have you found?" Sally asked.

Jason stared at the photo intently. "Xavier's weakness."

"And what exactly is that?"

Jason turned to face her. "Xavier *thinks* he's a great racer."

THE CHALLENGER RACE

LAP: 13 OF 30

The Challenger Race was run at a blistering pace—if you took a turn an inch too wide, you were overtaken by the car behind you. If you missed a turn by a few yards, *three* drivers would shoot past you.

You also had to take into account the constantly falling rain of confetti in the city sections of the course—it made the air misty, cloudy, affecting visibility. The bullet-paced cars left spiraling snow-trails of the shredded paper in their wakes.

The Challenger course was a supertight track that twisted and turned through Greater New York—from the home straightaway on Fifth Avenue, out to JFK

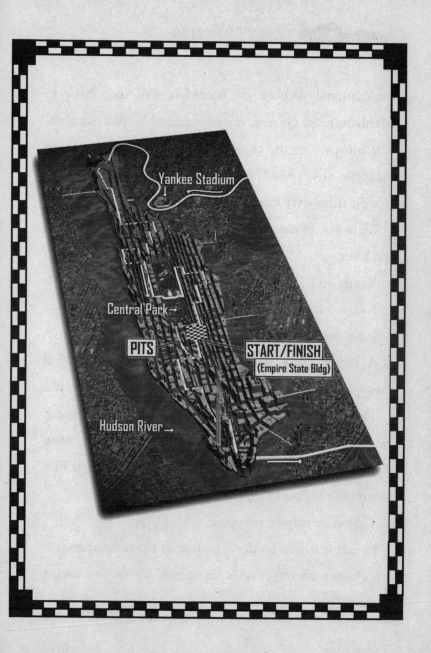

International Airport via Brooklyn, and then back to Manhattan via Queens, the Bronx, and Yankee Stadium. The intricacy of the course made it especially tough on magneto drives—each racer would require no less than five pit stops over thirty relatively short laps.

Right out of the gates, two drivers had zoomed out to the front.

Xavier and Jason.

Xavier had gone straight into the lead.

Jason had tucked in close behind him.

A larger chase pack of ten racers loomed behind them—with Ariel and Varishna Krishna embedded in it.

Then, on the third lap of the race, as the chase pack came roaring down the home straightaway, the nasty Russian twins, Igor and Vlad Krotsky, claimed their first victim: the Indian racer, Chandra.

The result was catastrophic.

In fact it would go down as one of the most spectacular chain-reaction crashes in recent hover car racing history.

Chandra had been leading the chase pack, and the Krotskys, in an attempt to push past him, had squeezed Chandra from either side, one hitting him on the front left side, the other pushing on Chandra's rear right flank, forcing him into a sideways lateral skid.

The problem was, Chandra—intent on winning this vital race—didn't give in.

And he made his biggest mistake. He powered up . . . and flipped . . . turning his car fully sideways into the wind and as such, he lost speed instantly—

Bam!

Bam!

Bam!

The next three racers slammed into him at full speed.

Carnage.

Hover cars flew every which way across Fifth Avenue.

Chandra's car hit the ground hard, crumpled against the asphalt—then Zhang Lao careered straight into it.

Ejection. Explosion.

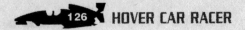

Varishna Krishna came next. Boxed in by two other racers, there was no way he could avoid the ugly pile of metal that was Chandra's and Lao's cars. He and his navigator ejected a nanosecond before the *Calcutta-IV* hit the pile and also became shrapnel.

The fourth and last car to hit the pile was Markos Christos's *Arion*. It banked to avoid the pile, but clipped it with its left wing, snapping the wing clean off—which caused the Greek racer to lose all control and shoom at right angles across Fifth Avenue and take out three more racers!

It was only the magnetic dead zone protecting the nearest building that stopped them all from smashing right through its windows.

The four cars hit the dead zone, stopped, then fell, dropping like shot birds down to the roadway.

The end result of this great conflagration was twofold.

First: The crash left two high piles of battered and crumpled hover cars on either side of Fifth Avenue, creating a kind of gateway between them, a gateway big enough for only one car to fit through at a time.

And second: It left Xavier Xonora and Jason Chaser well clear of the rest of the field.

The New York Challenger Race, winner take all, was now a two-horse race.

THE CHALLENGER RACE
LAP: 18 OF 30

Xavier and Jason.

Out in front.

On their own.

Engaged in the race of their lives.

Left and right, they weaved through the city section of the track. Then blasting out through the streets of Brooklyn, before shooting up and down the runways at JFK, slowing dramatically at the ultrasharp hairpins there.

And all the while, Xavier drove perfectly, never once giving Jason a chance to get past him.

Jason hung in there, only a few car-lengths behind the *Speed Razor*.

On each lap, he actually *gained* on Xavier in the super-tight city section of the course just before the home straightaway—banking left and right in the confetti-filled canyons of New York City—but in the straight-line sections of the track, Xavier would power away from him, canceling out the gains Jason had made.

The situation was all too familiar.

No matter what he tried, Jason just couldn't get past the Black Prince. He was half a second behind Xavier, but it might as well have been half an hour.

Lap 20 went by, and still Xavier remained in front.

Lap 25—and Jason was still on his tail.

He's just too good! Jason's mind screamed. *Too good! But that's also his weakness: He thinks he's too darn good.*

"Sally!" Jason called into his radio. "Time to start the plan! You ready?"

"You're absolutely crazy, superstar," came the reply, *"which is why I love you so much. Let's dance."*

Jason flew around the next lap—Lap 26—like a bullet, hanging on to Xavier's tail, but if anything, compared to

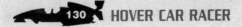

his previous laps, it looked like Jason had actually lost ground to Xavier.

He had.

"*Okay!*" Sally called. "*You just lost a second to Xavier on that lap!*"

"One second is okay," Jason said grimly. "I hope Oliver Koch noticed."

Lap 27—and Jason lost more ground to Xavier.

"*Another half second . . . ,*" Sally called. "*He's pulling away from you!*"

It was true. Xavier was pulling away from him—even the crowd could see it now.

But that was part of the plan. It could only work if Xavier *thought* he was pulling away from Jason.

And with only three laps remaining, the race looked over.

It was Xavier out in front.

Then Jason.

Then daylight, thanks to the big crash, followed by the Russians and Ariel Piper.

Lap 28—and Xavier was ahead of Jason by two full seconds.

In the pits, Sally looked over at Oliver Koch—the *Speed Razor*'s mech chief was looking at his race computer and speaking into his radiomike.

"Oliver's taking the bait, Jason," she reported.

"He should be taking the bait," Jason said. *"It was this kind of attention to detail that won him Mech Chief of the Year. Now it's gonna lose him this race."*

Lap 29—and the lead extended another 0.2 of a second.

Sally took a deep breath. "I hope you're right about this, Jason," she whispered.

And with that the last lap began.

At the start of the final lap, Xavier's lead over Jason was a full 2.2 seconds. Even if Jason hauled him in amid the city S-bends near the home straightaway, he'd only gain a second.

Xavier was out of reach.

But then a strange thing happened.

As soon as the last lap began, Jason started gaining on Xavier—just slowly, in a measured way, over the course of the entire lap.

They hit JFK and the lead was 2.0 seconds.

Up through Queens and it was 1.7 seconds.

Then over the East River and down through the Bronx and the lead was down to 1.5 seconds.

The Bug said something.

"I know! I know!" Jason said. "If I'm right, this one's gonna go right down to the wire. That's what I'm banking on! The home straightaway *on the last lap* is the only place I can get him!"

Then the two cars swept around Yankee Stadium and headed south, into the confetti-filled canyons of the city for the last time.

And here Jason made his move.

As he'd done the entire race, he gained on Xavier amid the right-angled turns of the city.

The gap between them narrowed quickly now:

1.2 seconds . . .

1.1 seconds . . .

1.0 second . . .

As he banked and swerved through the buildings of the Upper West Side, Jason saw the *Speed Razor* through the veil of falling confetti—saw it getting nearer and nearer.

Hopefully Xavier was expecting this, having seen it the whole race.

And that was the key, Jason thought. This was all about what Xavier expected.

Then the two leaders shot across Central Park at the 79th Street Transverse—and when they blasted out of Central Park on the Fifth Avenue side, the lead was half a second.

Now there were only about twenty seconds of racing left. They came down through the Upper East Side, through the confetti snow, Xavier taking turns perfectly—impossible to pass—Jason edging closer.

And then the final turn onto Fifth Avenue came into view.

"Here we go . . . ," Jason said.

The *Speed Razor* and the *Argonaut* hit the left-hander almost together.

As they did so, Jason swung in low, lower than usual, diving through the confetti, looking like he was going to go under the *Speed Razor*.

But he wasn't going under it—he was just aiming for its blind spot, and with all the confetti floating around, Xavier's navigator was more blind than usual.

The two cars hit the straightaway.

And then Xavier did it.

Just as Jason had hoped.

A thousand feet short of the Finish Line, he punched his fist into the air in triumph.

Just as he had done in each of his victories at the Sponsors' Tournament.

And at the Italian Run.

And whenever he'd won a race at Race School.

Xavier, as Jason had noticed during their study sessions, had a habit of celebrating prematurely.

As so, at that moment, Jason jammed every thruster forward.

It made for an astonishing sight.

Xavier in the *Speed Razor*, roaring down Fifth Avenue to the cheers of the crowds, blasting through the confetti rain, with his fist thrown into the air in triumph . . .

. . . before suddenly, there was the *Argonaut,* zipping alongside him from out of nowhere!

And as the two cars came to the crumpled piles of broken cars on either side of the home straightaway, Jason darted ahead of Xavier and whip-weaved quickly in front of him!

The crowd gasped at the audacity of it.

Xavier's eyes boggled.

And the *Argonaut* roared through the narrow gap

From out of nowhere

between the two piles of smashed-up hover cars and shot like a rocket across the Finish Line.

In.

First.

Place.

It was the photo that had done it.

The photo from Jason's only victory over Xavier Xonora—his photo-finish win in Race 25.

Gazing closely at the photo the evening before the Challenger Race, Jason had seen something very peculiar in it.

Whereas before he had only ever seen the nose of the *Argonaut* sneaking across the Finish Line inches ahead of the *Speed Razor*, on this occasion, he had seen something else entirely.

There in the photo, frozen forever in that moment in time, Jason had seen Xavier's fist punching the air.

Xavier, thinking he had won when in fact he had not, had prematurely pumped his fist into the sky.

And so Jason had formulated his plan—he would use Xavier's perfect pit crew against him, allow them to feed Xavier information about his increasing lead, *and then on the last lap Jason would pounce*. He would gain on Xavier over the course of the final lap and then overtake him *on the home straightaway*, the one place Xavier dropped his guard, the one place on a race course where he was vulnerable.

The New York crowds roared with both delight and disbelief at such a daring strategy.

Jason had caught everyone by surprise.

By the time he swung into the pits, every television crew in the city was camped outside his pit bay.

After a well-earned team hug with Sally and the Bug behind the closed doors of their garage, he came out to face the media.

"Jason! Jason! Did you plan it from the start?"

"Jason! How did you know Xavier would make such a rookie mistake?"

"Jason! How does it feel to know that you just qualified for the New York Masters?"

It was the last question that caught Jason short.

"It feels . . . great," he said. "Only I . . . I don't have a licensed team to sponsor me. And without a team, I can't race."

"You can race under my name anytime, my young friend!" a familiar voice boomed from somewhere nearby.

Umberto Lombardi stood behind the assembled media throng, grinning from ear to ear.

He spread his arms wide. "I used to have a second car, but some young driver destroyed it in Italy earlier this year! If you're prepared to race in your own car, young Jason, you can race under my licence in the Masters Series!"

The media swung their microphones to Jason.

But just as Jason was about to answer, another voice rose above the throng.

"I have another suggestion," the voice said.

Everyone turned—

—to see a very well-dressed man in a suit standing beside Lombardi. He was younger than Lombardi, mid-forties, American, with perfectly groomed hair, and he wore a suit that screamed money.

He was one of the most well-known figures in racing.

He was Antony Nelson, head of the Lockheed-Martin Factory Team.

"For I *do* have a spare car," Nelson said imperiously. "My team was ready to run a third car in the Masters, but sadly, our first-choice racer"—he glanced across at Xavier's pit bay—"didn't make the grade in the Challenger. You did, Mr. Chaser. As such, the Lockheed-Martin Racing Team would be honored if you would race for us in the New York Masters Series."

The offer hung in the air.

The media people froze, their eyes locked on Jason.

Alone on the stage, Jason gazed out over the crowd of reporters and photographers—saw their eager hungry faces, hungry for the story.

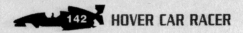

Then he looked at Nelson and Lombardi—and found a study in contrasts. One small and slick, the other broad and loud. One had a top-tier car waiting for him, the other had nothing but an International Racing Federation License.

And one had eaten greasy chicken burgers with Jason . . . and the other, quite obviously, hadn't eaten a chicken burger in years.

Jason took a deep breath.

"I think I'll race with Team Lombardi."

The media huddle erupted—with shouted questions and flash photos, but Jason was done.

He just stepped back into his pit bay, ignoring them, ending the press conference. He looked at his team: the diminutive Bug, the smiling Sally McDuff, and the serious Scott Syracuse.

"Well, people," he said. "I don't think I believe it yet myself. But in two days' time, we're gonna be racing in the New York Masters."

• • •

Thirty minutes later, the media throng had departed, having gotten their story, and Jason found himself standing in his pit bay, alone, tidying up after the race.

Across the way from him, he saw Xavier, also alone, also packing up his gear.

For some reason that he didn't understand, Jason went over to him.

"Good race today, Xavier," he said.

Xavier didn't even acknowledge Jason's presence, just kept packing.

"Okay, then . . ." Jason turned to go.

"By any reckoning, I'm a better racer than you are," Xavier's voice said from behind him.

Jason turned back.

Xavier was glaring at him now, his eyes icy. "All year it's been apparent. My speed tolerances are better. My cornering. My passing. My crew. In every facet of racing, *I am better than you are*. Which is why I cannot understand how on earth you beat me today. I should be racing in the Masters."

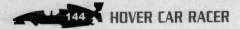

Jason just stared back at him, held his ground.

"You know why I beat you today, Xavier?"

"Why?"

"Because of everything you just said. You *are* better than me. You have heaps more natural talent than I do. *But I work harder than you do.* That's why I won. And that's why you've been scared of me all year—that's why you sent Dido to distract me, that's why you sent her to get information on me. And that's why, Prince Xavier, if we ever meet again on a racetrack, *I'll beat you there, too.* Have a nice life."

And with that, Jason turned his back on Xavier and walked away.

NEW YORK CITY, USA (WEDNESDAY)
PARADE DAY

The floats worked their way down Fifth Avenue, bearing on their backs the sixteen racers who would compete in the Masters.

All of New York had come out to see them. The streets of the city were lined with over ten million people, waving and throwing streamers. Ticker tape fell from the upper heights of the skyscrapers, mingling with the ever-present confetti snow.

Jason, Sally, and the Bug stood atop a gigantic papier-mâché float—built in the shape and colors of the *Argonaut*—waving to the cheering crowds.

On the other floats, Jason saw some familiar faces.

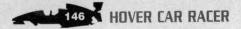

Alessandro Romba.

La Bomba Romba. The current world champion and, this year, the winner in Sydney, London, and Italy. If he won the Masters this week, he'd become the first racer ever to win the Golden Grand Slam, all four Grand Slam races in a single calendar year.

And on another float: Fabian.

The nasty Frenchman whom Jason—via Ariel—had humiliated in the exhibition race in Italy.

Etienne Trouveau—Fabian's equally villainous team-mate—the man who had taken out Jason's tailfin so ruthlessly in Italy.

And the two U.S. Air Force pilot-racers, Angus Carver and Dwayne Lewicki—the crowd gave them a huge cheer.

At one point during the parade, Jason made eye contact with Fabian.

The Frenchman smiled at him, and then formed his fingers into a gun and—his smile vanishing—pulled the trigger.

●　●　●

While Jason and the others were out on Fifth Avenue, the *Argonaut*—the tough little *Argonaut*—sat in a Team Lombardi pit bay on Sixth Avenue being overhauled.

Umberto Lombardi may not have been able to give Jason a brand-new, race-ready car to compete in the Masters, but, as he had done in Italy, he could give the *Argonaut* a bit of an upgrade: some brand-new compressed-air thrusters, another new tailfin, and a crate-load of the best magneto drives money could buy— Ferrari XP-7s.

No longer was the *Argonaut* a hodgepodge of wildly different parts—now, internally at least, it was the complete package.

Externally, however, Lombardi didn't change a thing.

The only thing he got his workmen to do on the outside of the car was give the *Argonaut* a complete repainting and polishing—not in the colors of Team Lombardi, but in its own original colors: blue, white, and silver.

When it came out of the garage later that afternoon—

when Jason and the others had returned from the parade—the *Argonaut* positively sparkled.

It was ready to race.

Throughout the rest of the day, Jason and his team stayed away from all the formal race functions—dinners, sponsors' events, drinks parties.

Having seen how vacuous those things were both in Italy and at Race School, Jason, Sally, and the Bug didn't care for them.

They just stayed at the official practice track out on Long Island Sound—putting the new-and-improved *Argonaut* through its paces—before returning to Jason's cousins' house in New Jersey late in the afternoon.

That evening, the entire extended Chaser family, the McDuff clan, Ariel Piper, and Scott Syracuse sat around the dinner table, discussing tactics.

"The important thing is the elimination system," Syracuse said. "Over the course of the four races, a scoreboard is used. Like at Race School, you get ten points for winning, down to one point for coming in tenth—and a flat zero points if you DNF. At the end of each race, the last four racers on the scoreboard get eliminated. So: in Race 1, sixteen racers compete; in Race 2, twelve; in Race 3, eight; and in the final race, only four.

"As such, the first race is simple," he said. "If you come in the last four, you're out. If you survive the first race, then elimination depends on everyone's scores in the subsequent races."

"And don't forget the Bradbury Principle," Henry Chaser, ever the armchair expert, said. His eyes twinkled as he said it.

"Yes, Dad," Jason sighed, shaking his head.

"Hey, look!" one of his cousins yelled from in front of the TV. "You can bet on Jason!"

Everyone turned to see that the TV news was reporting on the gambling odds being offered for the Masters. A representative from the main Internet gambling company, InterBet, was summarizing the available odds.

Jason was a rank outsider to win the Masters—his odds were the highest of any racer: 1,500-to-1.

But what surprised Jason was the amount of different betting options that were available to the keen gambler:

You could bet on Jason making it through Race 1 (100-to-1).

You could bet on him making it to Race 4 (575-to-1).

But then there were the more complex bets.

Jason coming in the top three overall.

Jason coming in the top five overall.

Jason placing in the top three in any race (naturally the odds for Race 1 were shorter than those for, say, Race 3, since he'd have to avoid eliminations to get to Race 3).

Jason placing in the top five in any race.

Jason was a little overwhelmed by it all. He'd always loved racing, but he'd never taken an interest in the gambling side of it.

"Hmmm. I'm not much of a gambler," Martha Chaser said tentatively, "but I might just put a dollar on you to win the whole thing. I could buy myself one of those fancy new sewing machines. Mmmm."

After a time, dinner broke up, and Jason and the Bug went to their bedroom. They wanted a good night's sleep before tomorrow's racing.

Before he climbed into bed, though, Jason had a thought—and he went online, checking something . . . something about the gambling odds on him in Italy.

Hmmm, he thought, gazing at the screen, before flicking it off.

Then his parents came in, wished him and the Bug good night, switched the lights off, and left.

Jason lay in the dark for a long time—long after the Bug had fallen silent—staring at the ceiling. Then he rolled over to go to sleep.

As he did so, someone came into the bedroom behind him and sat down on the floor between his bed and the Bug's.

It was their father, Henry Chaser.

"Boys," he whispered, assuming they were asleep. "I

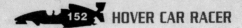

just wanted you both to know something. I am so very proud of you—not for reaching the Masters, but just for being who you are and conducting yourselves as you have. Tomorrow, win or lose, it doesn't matter, I still love you both. You just do your best and enjoy the experience. I hope you have the time of your lives."

Henry sniffed back some tears.

Then he stood up quickly and left the room.

Jason smiled in his bed.

He didn't know it, but across from him, in the other bed, the Bug was also wide awake and listening.

Lightning speed.

Blurring skyscraper canyons.

Slow-falling confetti.

Roaring crowds.

And absolutely *brutal* racing.

Race 1 of the New York Masters introduced Jason to a whole new level of hover car racing.

This wasn't just *fast*.

It was desperate. You did everything you could to stay out of the bottom four . . . and stay alive.

The course for the Liberty Supersprint wasn't dissimilar

NEW YORK MASTERS
RACE 1:
LIBERTY SUPERSPRINT
New York, USA

Course

Yankee Stadium

Queens

Hudson River

Brooklyn

NEW YORK

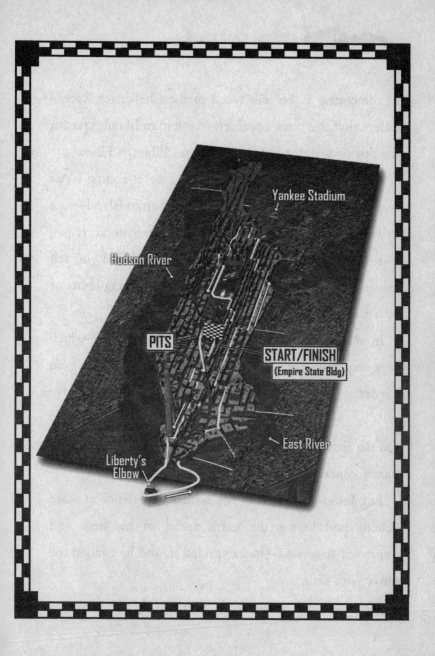

Yankee Stadium

Hudson River

PITS

START/FINISH
(Empire State Bldg)

East River

Liberty's
Elbow

to the course Jason had raced in the Challenger Race—except that this track never left Manhattan Island, save for the downward run to the treacherous Liberty's Elbow.

But this course was *tight*, sharp, a never-ending series of right-angle turns up and down Manhattan Island—as a driver, you never got a chance to rest your mind. If you lost your concentration for a second, you'd find yourself missing a turn and skidding out over the demag lights or into a dead zone.

In short, Race 1 was murder on mag drives—which was very deliberate. It made taking Liberty's Elbow even harder.

On the first corner of the race, Etienne Trouveau made a barely concealed swipe at Jason's tailfin.

But Jason—wiser from his similar experience at Race School and loving the extra speed of his new and improved *Argonaut*—had expected it, and he evaded the move with skill.

Welcome back to the big leagues was the message.

Twisting, turning, banking, racing.

Sixteen racers, but only twelve could progress to Race 2.

Fabian shot to the lead—

Closely pursued by La Bomba Romba—

Jason slotted into fourteenth place, racing hard, yet within range of elimination.

But he liked this course. It suited the light and nimble *Argonaut*. The never-ending sequence of short straightaways and 90-degree turns suited the smaller cars—in the city, there wasn't a single street section long enough for the heavier big-thruster cars to gather any straight-line speed.

Where they gained a slight advantage was on the short straightaway leading down to Liberty's Elbow.

And that was where things got hairy.

LAP: 17 OF 40

On Lap 17, Liberty's Elbow claimed her first victim.

Kamiko Ideki, running on worn mags at the back of the

field and hoping to pit at the end of that lap, lost control taking the notorious left-hand hairpin.

He lost it wide, understeering badly, and pushing his struggling mags to the max, he blew them and flipped—

—and rolled wildly—

—tumbling out of the turn, heading at phenomenal speed toward one of the giant horseshoe-shaped hover grandstands that lined the corner, before he was caught— abruptly, instantly—like a fly in a spider's web in the protective dead zone enveloping the Elbow.

Out of the race, Kamiko would now automatically be eliminated.

LAP: 32 OF 40

Into the pits. Frantic activity everywhere.

And Sally did well, very well, sending Jason out ahead of two racers who'd actually entered the pits *before* him—Raul Hassan, the number-two driver for the Lockheed-Martin Team, and Jason's Lombardi teammate, Pablo Riviera—the

The notorious left-hand hairpin

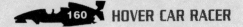

in-pit passing maneuver elevating Jason to twelfth.

He felt a little relieved—with Ideki already out, as long as he didn't come thirteenth, fourteenth, or fifteenth, he'd be returning for Race 2.

But as the race entered its final stages, things were about to get nasty.

LAP: 35 OF 40

Raul Hassan in his Lockheed tried to overtake Jason at the Elbow.

After Jason's in-pit passing on Lap 32, Hassan had hounded him for the next three laps, snapping at Jason's heels—so that when they hit the Elbow on Lap 35, they hit it almost together.

The two cars banked sharply, side by side, Jason on the inside, Hassan on the outside.

Jason felt the immense G-forces of the turn assaulting his body. He gripped his steering wheel for dear life, as if it were the only thing holding him inside the *Argonaut*.

The G-force meter on his dashboard ticked upward:

6.2 . . .

7.1 . . .

8.0 . . .

And then—just as Hassan had planned—it happened.

For the briefest of instants, as his car hit 8-Gs, Jason
blacked out.

A squeal from the Bug roused him—

—and he decelerated, wrestling with his steering wheel,
and caught the *Argonaut* just before it hit the dead zone—

—but not before Hassan, Riviera, and a third driver,
Carlo Martinez in a Boeing-Ford, all snuck past Jason.

It was a costly mistake.

Suddenly the *Argonaut* was coming in fifteenth place.

Suddenly Jason was coming in last.

LAP: 36 OF 40

The last four laps of the race went by in a blur.

Jason raced as though his life depended on it, zigging

and zagging through the tight New York streets.

Yet his error at the Elbow had hurt him—on every lap, he took it ever more gingerly . . . and he gradually fell farther behind the others.

But he kept on driving anyway, keeping them in sight, staying close.

Something could happen.

Anything could happen.

So long as you were there at the end, you had a chance.

This was Henry Chaser's "Bradbury Principle," in reference to that time at the Winter Olympics when the Australian short-track speedskater, Steven Bradbury, had dropped back behind the leaders, only to see them *all* fall—taking each other out in a spectacular crash—on the final turn of the race.

As all the lead skaters lay splayed everywhere on the ice, Bradbury had simply skated past them and won the gold, incidentally the first gold medal Australia had ever won at a Winter Olympic Games.

The Bradbury Principle: Stay alive and you never knew.

And in Masters racing, it had particular relevance: Year after year, the final laps of each race saw some of the most downright dangerous driving ever, as racers sought to avoid elimination at any cost.

This reckless driving was so common, it had a name: Masters Madness.

LAP: 40 OF 40

Into the last lap, and Jason was lagging behind the next five racers by about six car-lengths.

Raul Hassan had moved up through the field, as had Pablo Riviera, both now well clear of the bottom three.

Immediately in front of Jason were:

In twelfth (and thus safe from elimination): Helmut Reitze, the German driver from the Porsche Team.

In thirteenth: Carlo Martinez, in his Boeing-Ford.

In fourteenth: Brock Peters, from the General Motors Team.

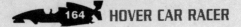

And then Jason.

Whipping through the financial district, and he couldn't haul them in.

Down to the Elbow, still no decent gain.

And then it was back up through the city, bending and banking furiously, before he crossed Central Park for the last time and came to the final few corners of the course.

Jason kicked himself for his earlier mistake, but strangely, he was happy.

He'd made it to the Masters.

And that in itself was an extraordinary achievement. He'd be back in future years, he was sure, but he'd be older then, wiser, a better racer. He was, after all, only fifteen.

And then, as the racers in front of him hit the final left-hand turn of the race he saw—spectacularly, gloriously—the Bradbury Principle in action.

It was largely the fault of the thirteenth-place racer, Carlo Martinez, as he tried to avoid elimination by over-taking the twelfth-place driver, Helmut Reitze, in his Porsche.

By any reckoning, there was no room to move, but Martinez tried anyway—Masters Madness—thrusting his Boeing inside Reitze's silver Porsche on the final turn.

The result was as tragic as it was spectacular.

Martinez collected Reitze—and the two cars rolled together, but not before the car immediately behind them, the GM of Brock Peters, slammed fully into the back of them. Peters and his navigator ejected an instant before their car disappeared in a billowing explosion of flames.

All three cars crashed to the roadway, their charred remains littering the final turn on both the left and right.

At which point, the *Argonaut*—left for dead in last place—just cruised by them, banking into Fifth Avenue, slicing past the dark columns of smoke rising from the wreckage, before it zoomed across the Finish Line, the last car to cross the Line in Race 1, but safely in twelfth place.

By sheer good fortune, by just hanging in there when all seemed lost, Jason had made it to Race 2!

NEW YORK CITY, USA (THURSDAY)
AFTER LIBERTY SUPERSPRINT

As soon as the Liberty Supersprint was over, gigantic scoreboards sprang to life across New York City: above the Start-Finish Line on Fifth Avenue, in Times Square, on the Brooklyn Bridge, and in hundreds of other locations.

The scoreboard looked like this:

DRIVER	LIBERTY SUPERSPRINT	MANHATTAN GATE RACE	THE PURSUIT	THE QUEST	TOTAL
1. **ROMBA, A. (1)** *Lockheed-Martin Racing*	10				10
2. **FABIAN (17)** *Team Renault*	9				9

DRIVER	LIBERTY SUPERSPRINT	MANHATTAN GATE RACE	THE PURSUIT	THE QUEST	TOTAL
3. TROUVEAU, E. (40) *Team Renault*	8				8
4. CARVER, A. (24) *USAF Racing*	7				7
5. LEWICKI, D. (23) *USAF Racing*	6				6
6. SKAIFE, M. (102) *General Motors Factory Team*	5				5
7. HASSAN, R. (2) *Lockheed-Martin Racing*	4				4
8. REIN, D. (45) *Boeing-Ford Team*	3				3
9. CHOW, A. (38) *China State Racing*	2				2
10. REITZE, R. (51) *Porsche Racing*	1				1
11. RIVIERA, P. (12) *Lombardi Racing Team*	0				0
12. CHASER, J. (55) *Lombardi Racing Team*	0				0
13. REITZE, H. (50) *Porsche Racing*	DNF				
14. MARTINEZ, C. (44) *Boeing-Ford Team*	DNF				

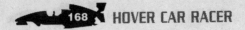
15. PETERS, B. (05)					
General Motors Factory Team	DNF				
16. IDEKI, K. (11)					
Yamaha Racing Team	DNF				

While Jason had been struggling at the back of the field, a fierce battle had been going on up front—between Alessandro Romba and the two Renault Team drivers: Fabian and Etienne Trouveau. In the end, Romba had held out the two Frenchmen and won, claiming ten points and inching one step closer to the Golden Grand Slam.

The last four drivers—all of them having crashed out during the race—were blocked out in red, eliminated.

After the next race, four more would be gone.

That night, Jason went to bed both exhausted and exhilarated. Sure, he was last on the scoreboard, but he had high hopes for the next day's race—for it was a gate race, his and the Bug's specialty.

As he slept, an army of workers went to work reconfiguring New York City—erecting arched gates and towering barricades—preparing it for the Manhattan Gate Race.

PERTH FINISH ...

... to the same time of today. Some how it gave ...
labored. Now, as I'm—switching around sides—the ...
character, I attacked—he passed it for the Manhattan ...

NEW YORK CITY, USA (FRIDAY)

Dawn on Friday found the streets of New York City eerily deserted. Not a single car, cab, or truck could be seen on any of its wide boulevards—vehicular traffic was banned today.

If you moved through those streets, however, you would find that many of them were now fitted with high metal archways—race gates—250 of them.

You would also find that dozens of the city's streets had been blocked off—by massive temporary barricades—transforming them into dead ends.

The island of Manhattan had been turned into a labyrinth.

Every year the configuration of New York's streets was

altered—racers and navigators would receive a map of all the gate locations and dead ends three minutes before racetime.

As with all gate races, the farthest gates were worth one hundred points; the nearest, ten. And since no racer could possibly race through every single gate within the time limit, this was a battle of strategy—choosing the optimal course.

The time limit for the race was three hours.

The punishment for a late return to the Start-Finish Area was severe: two points *per second*.

So if you were a minute late, you lost a massive 120 points.

The Manhattan Gate Race was also the only race in the New York Masters to operate under the "Car Over the Line" finishing rule. Driver Over the Line wasn't good enough in this race—your whole car had to make it back.

The message was clear: Go out, get through as many gates as you could, and get back on time.

• • •

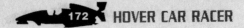

Jason arrived in the pit area on Sixth Avenue very early on Friday morning.

Nervous, he'd slept fitfully and woken terribly early, around 4:30 a.m., so he'd decided to go down to the pits and tinker with the *Argonaut*.

He was looking inside its rear thrusters when a voice behind him made him jump:

"Ooh, hello there! Why, if it isn't young Jason."

It was Ravi Gupta. The slightly creepy Indian fellow Jason had met in Italy—whom Jason had subsequently discovered was a leading bookmaker.

Gupta stood a few yards away from Jason, with his hands clasped peacefully in front of him—but he had arrived all but silently, as if he had apparated out of thin air.

"What are you doing in here?" Jason asked. "This area is restricted."

"Ooh, I have been involved in racing for a long time, Jason," Gupta said slyly. "I know people."

"What do you want?"

Gupta held up his hands quickly. "Me? Ooh, nothing, Jason. Nothing at all. I thought you were lucky yesterday— ooh, yes, very very lucky—with that crash on the last turn."

"A race is never over until everyone crosses the line," Jason said warily.

"Yes, ooh yes. So true, so true," Gupta said. "But now the simple fact of the matter is that you are in Race 2, the gate race, and everyone knows how much you like gate races. Feeling confident, then?"

Jason didn't like talking to Gupta—it was as if Gupta was plying him for information, looking for the inside scoop on how he would perform that day, so he could adjust his betting odds accordingly.

Too late Jason had realized that this had been exactly what Gupta had done in Italy.

Smiling, Gupta said, "Enjoying your new and improved *Argonaut*. I must say it looks a million dollars."

"It's great," Jason said.

A door slammed somewhere. Jason turned. Saw a security guard walking down the length of the pits.

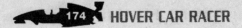

Jason swung back to address Gupta—

—only to find that the Indian had disappeared.

Vanished.

As suddenly and silently as he had arrived.

Jason scowled. "Hmmm . . ."

By 8 a.m., New York City was once again snowing with confetti.

The city was absolutely overflowing with spectators.

They lined every street, hung from office windows, lay on deck chairs on rooftops. Sizable crowds gathered around the two one-hundred-point gates in the Cloisters (at the extreme north of the island) and at the Brooklyn end of the long Brooklyn-Battery Tunnel (the southernmost point of the course), ever hopeful that this would be the year that a racer claimed both one-hundred-pointers.

But by far the largest crowd of all lined Fifth Avenue: an unbroken multitude that stretched from the New York Public Library on 42nd Street all the way down Fifth Avenue to the four-way Start-Finish Line that stood beneath the Empire State Building at the junction of Fifth and 34th Street.

The stage was set.

The crowd was ready.

The race would begin at 9 a.m.

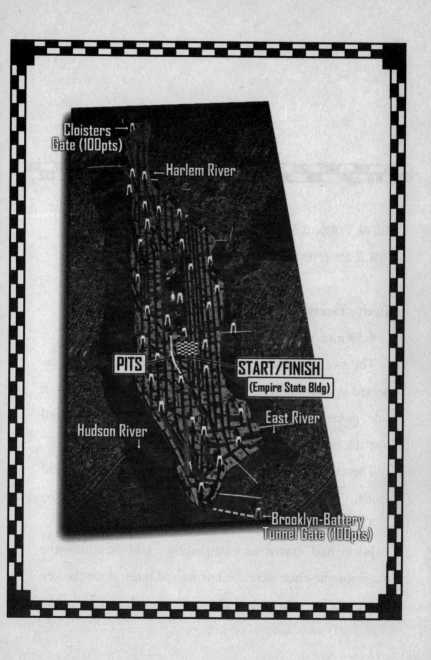

Cloisters
Gate (100pts)

Harlem River

PITS

START/FINISH
(Empire State Bldg)

East River

Hudson River

Brooklyn-Battery
Tunnel Gate (100pts)

NEW YORK CITY, USA (FRIDAY)
RACE 2: THE MANHATTAN GATE RACE

Twelve racers. 250 gates. Three hours.

8:59 a.m.

The twelve remaining racers in the Masters Series sat poised on the square-shaped Start-Finish Line, three to a side, pointing in the four cardinal directions—their initial starting direction determined by lot.

Then the clock struck 9:00 and—*bam*—the lights went green.

They were off.

Jason had drawn an east-pointing grid position—the most sought-after were the northward ones, since the key point-scoring area was in the mid-to-north section of the island—and while all the racers around him blasted off to the east and then turned north, he just swung around completely *on the spot* and—at the Bug's instruction—darted due south down Fifth Avenue, heading for the southern half of the island.

But one other driver also headed south, staying close behind Jason.

Fabian.

And as Jason weaved his way southward, whizzing through the picture-postcard gates at Washington Square Park, the World Trade Center Memorial, and Wall Street, it quickly became apparent that Fabian hadn't just followed Jason southward.

Fabian was following Jason everywhere.

Every single time Jason turned for a new gate, Fabian turned after him.

"Goddarnit, Bug!" Jason yelled. "He's tailing us! He doesn't trust his own navigator, so he's using our race plan!"

Tailing in a gate race (in the southern hemisphere it was

called *sequencing*) wasn't unheard of: It was technically within the rules, but it was also regarded as a cheap and cowardly way to race.

All the way down Manhattan, the crowds cheered the *Argonaut* on . . .

. . . cheers that became boos as the purple and gold *Marseilles Falcon* shot by a split second later.

Through more gates at the southwestern corner of the island. Every time the *Argonaut* passed through an archway, that gate emitted a shrill electronic ping:

Bing! Bing! Bing!

The Bug's race plan was near perfect—plotted to pass through the maximum number of worthwhile gates while bypassing those that offered only minimal points for inordinate effort.

And all the while, he kept Jason close enough to the pits for necessary mag replacements and coolant refuelings.

By the time they took their second pit stop at the one-hour mark, the *Argonaut* was sitting on an incredible 750 points—and in the lead!

Unfortunately, Fabian—because he was following exactly the same course—had the same number of points and thus shared the lead.

But then Jason did something unexpected.

He went south again, this time taking the superfast route down the FDR.

He was going for the Brooklyn-Battery Tunnel. And the prized one-hundred-point gate at its end.

Fabian visibly doubted whether or not to follow, but in the end, he did.

In hindsight, it was a very canny plan—take on the tunnel with six full-strength mags, a full tank of coolant, and no distractions.

The Brooklyn-Battery Tunnel came into view, and without missing a beat, the *Argonaut* shoomed into it, closely followed by the *Marseilles Falcon*.

A minute later, Jason emerged at the turnaround at the other end of the long tunnel—the Brooklyn end—to be met by the roars of the crowd gathered there, and he banked hard, swooping through the one-hundred-point gate . . .

Bing!

. . . before he roared back into the tunnel to start the return journey.

But while Jason was plundering the southern areas, others were progressing well in the northern half of the island.

Chief among them were the two USAF racers: Carver and Lewicki.

They were gate race specialists, the U.S. Air Force priding itself on its pilots' abilities to most efficiently navigate any course.

Word was, Carver and Lewicki's Air Force navigators trained on state-of-the-art computer navigation simulators for ten hours a day, so that optimal race plotting became almost second nature to them.

But when it was revealed at the one-hour mark that at 740 points each, they were both ten points behind the leaders, Jason and Fabian, the crowds and the commentators went wild.

The television commentators—with the help of their

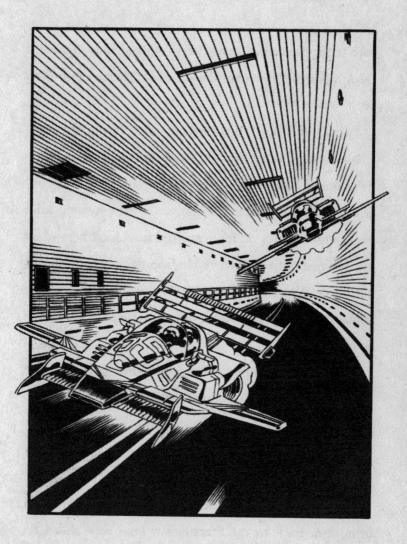

Back into the tunnel

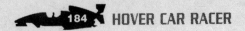

own course-plotting computers—immediately analyzed Jason's possible race plans based on his course-plotting so far.

"Check this out," one of them said. "From the start, Chaser went south, while everyone else went north. Now he's coming back north, where the streets aren't as congested with other racers anymore, and he's stealing solid twenty-point gates on his way. And now look here—he's just jumped onto the Henry Hudson Parkway, still heading north. Now where could he be heading? Okay, here comes the computer's assessment of his plan. . . . What the hell—?"

The same thing happened on every other sports channel. Shocked commentators saw the Bug's plan.

"No way!"

"He can't be serious!"

"The computer must be wrong. . . ."

"No, it's working all right . . . and, holy Toledo, it'd bring him back to the Start-Finish Line way ahead on points, easily in first place! Folks, according to our race plan computer, Jason Chaser, the popular young racer in Car No.55, is going for the Cloisters. He's going for the one-hundred-point double! And, by God, if he makes it, according to our calculations, he's gonna win this race, too!"

RACETIME: 1 HOUR 30 MINS

At the halfway mark, the top five racers on the scoreboard were:

	DRIVER	NO.	CAR	POINTS
1.	CHASER, J.	55	*Argonaut*	1,250
2.	FABIAN	17	*Marseilles Falcon*	1,250
3.	CARVER, A.	24	*Mustang-I*	1,220
4.	LEWICKI, D.	23	*Mustang-II*	1,210
5.	ROMBA, A.	1	*La Bomba*	1,160

Jason was racing well—fast and hard—but it was the Bug who was having the race of his life. Word of his daring plan had spread, and race fans all over New York were on the edges of their seats, wondering if the *Argonaut* could possibly complete the double *and* win the race.

But Fabian stayed with him. And in the southern part of the course, the two U.S. Air Force racers were now accumulating points very well. It was also widely known that Alessandro Romba, the world champion, intensely disliked gate races—he would be thrilled if he retained his fifth placing in this race.

Elsewhere, other things were happening.

As the race entered its last hour, racers again began to get desperate, and they started taking more risks, started taking corners more recklessly—and when two speeding hover cars hit the same intersection from different directions, catastrophe could occur.

It was one such collision that took the Chinese racer, Au Chow, out of the race. He'd been in seventh place when he'd come blasting out of Central Park— just as one of the other tail-enders, the American Dan Rein in his Boeing-Ford, had been zooming down Fifth Avenue to pit.

The two cars clashed at right angles—with Rein careering spectacularly through Chow's nosewing, shearing the

Chinese racer's entire nosecone clean off, in the process almost taking Chow's legs off.

Rein came out of it with a crumpled nose, but he managed to limp back to the pits. Chow's race was over—and since he'd only garnered two miserable points in Race 1, so was his time in the Masters.

RACETIME: 2 HOURS 45 MINS

"I like your style, Bug!" Jason yelled as the *Argonaut* roared up Riverside Drive, occasionally ducking inland to plunder some forty-point gates on the high Upper West Side—all the while with Fabian hammering on their tail.

"Everyone thinks you're this sweet little mousy guy, but I always knew you were a glory seeker!" Jason said. "Only you could come up with a race plan that's points-heavy and history-making!"

The Bug replied with three words.

Jason nodded. "Death or glory. You bet your ass, little brother."

Up and up they went, zooming northward toward the Cloisters, their race now an equation of distance and time.

The one-hundred-point Cloisters Gate was the single farthest point on the course from the Start-Finish Line, and they had fifteen minutes left in this race.

But the Bug had planned well—basing his decision on the distance to the Cloisters, their speed, the big points available, and the ever-diminishing state of their mags. He'd planned it down to the second.

But there was still the Fabian issue.

Try as he might, Jason just couldn't shake Fabian.

The wily Frenchman was clinging to his tail, riding on the Bug's brilliant strategy—no doubt informed by his pit crew that it was a winning one.

A couple of times, Jason tried to lose Fabian in the maze of the Upper West Side, but to no avail.

And then, as the race clock hit 2:45 and Jason set his course for the Cloisters, Fabian did it for him.

Either he lost his nerve or he took a call on his radio to try a new plan—most observers thought he lost his nerve.

Whatever the reason, Fabian pulled off Riverside, swinging right, and headed back down toward Midtown—not prepared to take the risk of going all the way up to the Cloisters; preferring to take the points from lesser gates and get back within the three-hour time limit.

Now the *Argonaut* shoomed northward, alone.

Heading for the Cloisters.

Jason gripped his wheel tightly as the minutes ticked by.

At 2:50 exactly, the *Argonaut* roared into the Cloisters, the crowd there rising in a delighted Mexican wave as it zoomed past them and—*bing!*—whipped through the archway there, collecting one hundred points for its trouble.

"Yee-ha!" Jason yelled.

The Bug whooped it up too.

"Right," Jason said. "Now it's time to get back."

RACETIME: 2 HOURS 52 MINS

Overcautious racers rushed back over the Start-Finish Line, finishing a full eight minutes early, determined to bank their hard-earned points and avoid penalties for returning late. It was conservative racing, but in gate races, you never knew. . . .

According to the Bug's plan, the return journey was to be swift and simple.

Zoom due south all the way down Central Park West, along the border of the park, and then swing onto Broadway as it angled in toward Midtown—collecting a couple of easy ten-pointers there—before turning onto 42nd Street and heading for Fifth Avenue.

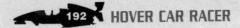

It was all going to plan until, at the very bottom of Central Park, the two Renaults of Fabian and Etienne Trouveau appeared from out of nowhere, slotting into identical positions on either side of the *Argonaut*.

Ostensibly, they were just other racers legitimately trying to get back home as fast as they could—but the way they buffeted the *Argonaut*, slashing at it with their razor-sharp bladed nosewings, Jason knew that this was something more.

They were trying to put him out of the race.

For good.

He held them off grimly, banging from one to the other, hemmed in on either flank, at one point roaring down Broadway on his side—but then as he turned left onto 42nd Street, only one right-hander away from home, the French racers got him.

The three cars took the left-hander onto 42nd Street together—with Fabian on the inside, Jason in the middle, and Trouveau on the outside.

And at that point, with cool calculation and in a manner

that just looked like vigorous racing, Fabian pushed Jason into Trouveau.

With nowhere else to maneuver, the *Argonaut* slid right, its nosewing coming closer and closer and closer to Trouveau's glistening bladed nosewing . . .

. . . and they hit.

CRACK!

The *Argonaut*'s nosewing splintered and broke and Jason lost all control.

The *Argonaut* veered downward, rushing toward the hard surface of 42nd Street—while the two Renaults flittered away like a pair of nasty ravens, their job done.

Jason somehow managed to pull his nose up and the *Argonaut* slammed into the roadway, landing awkwardly on its belly, right on top of its magneto drives.

Mags flew left and right, out from under the bouncing car: one, two, three, four of them . . .

. . . and the *Argonaut*—once beautiful, now battered and smoking—slid to a screeching halt in the middle of 42nd Street, one turn and 1,500 feet away from the Finish Line.

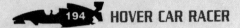

RACETIME: 2 HOURS 56 MINUTES

The crowd in the grandstand closest to the crashed *Argonaut* sighed with dismay at the unexpected crash.

The commentators on TV went bananas:

"Oh, no! Chaser is down! Chaser is down—!"

"Ladies and gentlemen, the race leader has crashed—!"

"And with only four minutes to go! In what could have been one of the best gate-race runs ever! Oh, the shame!"

Fabian and Trouveau both swung right, onto Fifth Avenue, and a few seconds later, roared over the Finish Line on 34th Street, eight blocks away.

The *Argonaut* sat nosedown—crumpled and broken—on 42nd Street, alongside the majestic New York Public Library.

Inside the stationary car, Jason raised his head weakly. The first thing he did was check behind him.

"You okay?"

The Bug groaned but nodded.

Jason keyed his power switch.

The *Argonaut*'s internal organs ticked over but did not catch. The car remained still.

Jason tried to start her up again. No luck.

"Come on, car!" Jason yelled. "Don't let me down! You've still got two mags! There's still time for us to get over the line!"

He keyed the power switch one last time.

Vmmm.

The *Argonaut* rose exactly two feet off the ground——and stayed there.

Jason pushed forward on his thrusters, but the car remained in a stationary hover—its compressed-air thrusters coughing pathetically—the car held up only by its two remaining magneto drives.

It had lost forward thrust.

The *Argonaut* wouldn't—couldn't—go forward.

Jason's face fell. If this had been a regular Masters race, he could have run for the Finish Line with his steering

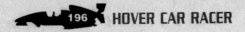

wheel, as the Bug had done back in Race 50 at Race School. But this was the only race in the Masters that was Car Over the Line: The *Argonaut* had to cross the line.

Jason looked up. "Oh *darn*."

RACETIME: 2 HOURS 57 MINS

With three minutes to go, eight of the twelve starters had crossed the Finish Line. Four remained out on the course: the crashed Au Chow; Raul Hassan, the second Lockheed-Martin driver; Dan Rein in his mended Boeing-Ford (both trying to get more points); and Jason.

At the time he crashed, Jason was in the lead on points.

But now, unmoving on 42nd Street, all agreed that his race was over.

The TV commentators overlooking the Finish Line bemoaned his crash.

"This is such a shame. . . ."

"Could have been a history-making drive. . . ."

· "But he's young, he'll learn. . . ."

"That's right, Bob, a gate race is never over until you're over that line."

But then, one of the commentators kicked back his chair and stood, pointing up Fifth Avenue, and raised his voice above them all:

"Wait a second! *What is that?*"

Every spectator on Fifth Avenue turned northward at the same time, and they all saw it together.

And for the first time in history, Fifth Avenue fell completely and utterly silent.

For what they saw totally took their breath away.

Through the glorious slow-motion confetti snow, they saw an object emerge from 42nd Street and come out onto Fifth Avenue.

It was the *Argonaut*.

Hovering low above the street.

And behind it, bent low with exertion, were two small figures.

Jason and the Bug were pushing it.

• • •

Slowly, gradually, with all their strength, Jason and the Bug pushed the *Argonaut* out onto Fifth Avenue.

The wide avenue stretched away before them—to the Finish Line, 1,500 feet away.

They kept pushing, and at first their slow journey proceeded in silence—the crowds massed in the stands on either side of them just watched them in sheer speechless shock.

And then someone yelled in a classic Noo York accent: "Come on, kids! Push that sucker home!"

And with those words, the spell was broken and the crowd exploded with applause and started urging Jason and the Bug on with roars that shook the heavens.

RACETIME: 2 HOURS 58 MINS

Two minutes to go. 660 feet to go.

Step by agonizing step, Jason and the Bug pushed the

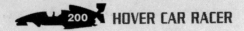

Argonaut—their *Argonaut*, their tough little car—down the home straightaway.

The crowds on either side of them were now in a frenzy, urging them on with rhythmic chants of:

"HEAVE! HEAVE!"

Sweat dripped off Jason's brow, splashed to the ground. The Bug leaned with all his might against the tailfin of the hovering *Argonaut*, pushing with his back.

The race clock ticked over to 2:59.

One minute to go.

But still 400 feet to travel and the boys were exhausted.

The commentators were abuzz with excitement:

". . . In all my years calling sports, I have *never* seen anything like this. . . ."

". . . We'll have to look at the points tally. Chaser was sixty points ahead of his nearest rival before he crashed. At this slow speed, he can't possibly get to the line before the three-hour mark. The question is: How many points will he lose for being late?"

The tiny figures of Jason and the Bug pushed their car

"Heave! Heave!"

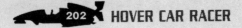

down Fifth Avenue, in front of the seething, cheering, roaring crowds in the multitiered grandstands.

"*HEAVE! HEAVE!*" came the chant.

Jason lowered his head, pushed.

Step, heave.

Step, heave.

But then, the Bug slipped . . . and fell.

Jason stopped, picked him up, put the Bug back where he had been standing.

"Keep pushing . . . !" he gasped. "We . . . have to . . . make it!"

And then the race-clock hit 3:00.

Every second now would cost them two points . . . and they still had 270 feet to go.

"*HEAVE . . . !*"

Twenty seconds gone.

"*HEAVE . . . !*"

Forty seconds gone.

"*HEAVE . . . !*"

A minute.

And then, seventy seconds after the three-hour time limit for the race had expired, to a million camera flashes exploding all around them, Jason Chaser and his brother, the Bug, pushed the *Argonaut* over the Finish Line and collapsed together in a heap.

Had he not wiped out on 42nd Street, Jason would have won the Manhattan Gate Race by sixty points—his dash to the Cloisters Gate would have made the difference.

As it turned out, however, with his seventy-second-late finish—incurring a whopping 140-point penalty—Jason ended up coming third, behind the two U.S. Air Force gate race specialists, Carver and Lewicki.

Fabian had come in fourth—aided by his early tailing of the *Argonaut*—and Romba was very satisfied to finish 5th.

But other results had gone Jason's way. The lesser-placed racers coming into the Gate Race—Hassan, Rein,

Chow, and Reitze—had either crashed (Chow), come in late (Hassan and Rein), or simply not fared well (Reitze), all of them coming in the bottom four.

Consequently, after the Gate Race the Masters Scoreboard looked like this:

DRIVER	LIBERTY SUPERSPRINT	MANHATTAN GATE RACE	THE PURSUIT	THE QUEST	TOTAL
1. **ROMBA, A. (1)** *Lockheed-Martin Racing*	10	6			**16**
2. **FABIAN (17)** *Team Renault*	9	7			**16**
3. **TROUVEAU, E. (40)** *Team Renault*	8	3			**11**
4. **CARVER, A. (24)** *USAF Racing*	7	10			**17**
5. **LEWICKI, D. (23)** *USAF Racing*	6	9			**15**
6. **SKAIFE, M. (102)** *General Motors Factory Team*	5	4			**9**
7. **HASSAN, R. (2)** *Lockheed-Martin Racing*	4	0			**4**
8. **REIN, D. (45)** *Boeing-Ford Team*	3	1			**4**
9. **CHOW, A. (38)** *China State Racing*	2	DNF			**2**
10. **REITZE, R. (51)** *Porsche Racing*	1	2			**3**
11. **RIVIERA, P. (12)** *Lombardi Racing Team*	0	5			**5**
12. **CHASER, J. (55)** *Lombardi Racing Team*	0	8			**8**

DRIVER	LIBERTY SUPERSPRINT	MANHATTAN GATE RACE	THE PURSUIT	THE QUEST	TOTAL
13. REITZE, H (50) *Porsche Racing*	DNF				
14. MARTINEZ, C (44) *Boeing-Ford Team*	DNF				
15. PETERS, B. (05) *General Motors Factory Team*	DNF				
16. IDEKI, K. (11) *Yamaha Racing Team*	DNF				

In one fell swoop, with his eight points for coming in third, Jason had leapfrogged over Hassan, Rein, Chow, and Reitze, not to mention his Lombardi teammate, Pablo Riviera.

He was now seventh in the overall points standings.

Which meant, incredibly, after two races, he was in the final eight racers.

Jason Chaser was still in the Masters.

And only two races away from glory . . .

PART III

JASON AND THE GOLDEN FLEECE

NEW YORK CITY, USA (SATURDAY)
RACE 3: THE PURSUIT
LAP 120 OF 120

The *Argonaut* screamed down the Hudson River at top speed, with Etienne Trouveau's *Vizir* right alongside it, banging against it, ramming it—on the very last lap of Race 3—and with only one turn to go, the fearsome Liberty's Elbow, Jason and Trouveau were out in front of the other racers, battling it out for the win.

The world blurred around Jason. The buildings of New York City. The bridges. The vast hover stands flanking the river.

This race had been bitter. Bitter and tough.

But now it had come to this—one turn, two racers.

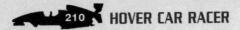

The *Argonaut* dived into the Elbow. So did the *Vizir*.

Jason battled the G-forces, gritted his teeth.

6-Gs . . .

The *Vizir* was still beside him.

7-Gs . . .

The *Argonaut* began to shake.

Jason gripped his steering wheel with all his might.

8-Gs and Jason's vision started to darken, the initial stages of blacking out.

Gotta stay conscious! he told himself. *Gotta stay conscious!*

But the *Vizir* was still beside him.

Worse, it was creeping *past* him, round the outside on the terrible turn!

How was Trouveau doing it? Jason's mind screamed.

8.5-Gs . . .

Jason started to feel nauseous. He'd never survived this many G-forces before—but all he could think of was the *Vizir* edging away from him, slipping out of his grasp, *beating him* in this race that he had to win to stay in the Masters.

Had to win.

Win.

Then the end of the giant hairpin came into view and—

—Jason blacked out.

The *Argonaut* was instantly flung clear of the Elbow.

Jason flopped back in his seat like a rag doll. Dimly, he heard the Bug scream in terror as their car rocketed out of control over the demag lights flanking the turn, screaming like a wounded fighter jet, before it flipped and bounced horribly on the surface of the harbor— pieces of it being stripped away in the process. Then the *Argonaut* slammed at tremendous speed into the carcass of another car that had crashed in the same manner earlier in the race and was blocking the nearest dead zone.

There was no chance to eject.

No chance of survival.

The *Argonaut* hit the wreck and exploded.

• • •

Jason awoke with a shout.

Jason awoke with a shout—dripping with sweat and breathless to the point of suffocation.

He caught his breath, and recognized his surroundings: He was in his cousin's bedroom in New Jersey. The Bug lay in the single bed beside his, snoring happily.

The digital clock next to Jason ticked over to 4:44 a.m.

It wasn't yet Saturday.

Race 3 had not been run.

It had just been a bad dream. A really bad dream.

But the emotions of it lingered: Jason's overwhelming desire to win, his pain at watching Trouveau pull away, the nausea of the G-forces, the descent into blackout, and worst of all, Jason's fear of that turn, Liberty's Elbow.

He just didn't like Liberty's Elbow—it was perhaps the toughest turn in racing—and today, like it or not, Jason was going to be taking it once every minute for two hours.

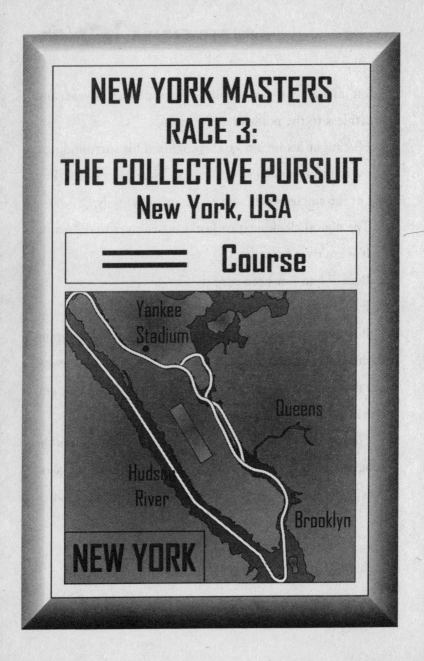

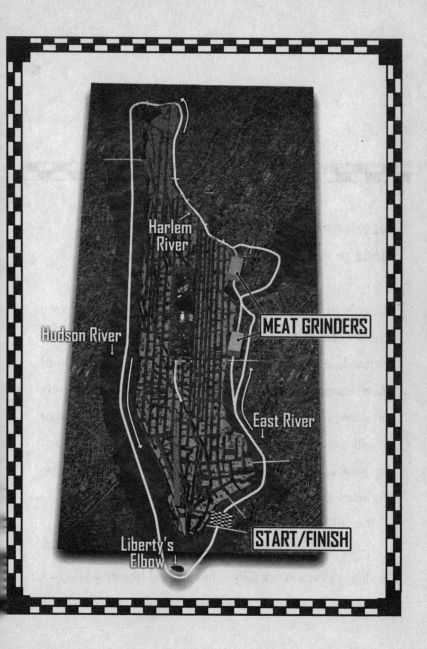

Harlem River

Hudson River

MEAT GRINDERS

East River

START/FINISH

Liberty's Elbow

NEW YORK CITY, USA (SATURDAY)
RACE 3: THE PURSUIT

Race 3 of the New York Masters is a variety of race known as a "Collective Pursuit Race."

Just like the pursuit races Jason had run in the school tournament, it involved racers blasting around a relatively short circular track—in Race 3, it was a lap of Manhattan Island, starting and ending at the Brooklyn Bridge. Each lap took approximately one minute, redefining the phrase "quicker than a New York Minute."

But this track featured obstacles:

First, *ion waterfalls* that rained down from all the bridges of New York City. They looked like upside-down fireworks displays: The luminescent gold particles of the ionized waterfalls wreaked havoc on magnetic and electrical systems. If you missed the one-car-wide gaps in the (moving) waterfalls, and accidentally drove your car *through* the falling curtain of golden ions, your car emerged on the other side as merely the shell of a hover car—no power, magnetic or electrical. A horrible crash usually ensued.

Second, *the Meat Grinders*: There are two forks in the pursuit course, at Roosevelt Island and at Ward's-Randall's Island (they are in fact one island, but were once two, hence the double name). At both forks, racers can take a longer, less dangerous route to the right-hand side.

The *left*-hand fork, however, is much shorter—but in both cases it contains an enormous iron wall, 200 feet thick, blocking the way completely. In the center of each iron wall is a narrow cylindrical tunnel. The thing is, the walls of this tunnel—the *entire* tunnel—open and close in an irislike fashion. If a racer chooses to take the short route, and gets caught in the closing tunnel, that racer can be crushed, hence the name "meat grinder." More often, desperate racers opt to take the short route, miss the opening of the tunnel, and lose even more time waiting for it to reopen.

And, of course, at the very end of each lap, at the end of the superlong and superfast Hudson River Straightaway, *Liberty's Elbow* loomed. It was the final challenge for every racer—pitting one's body against one's desire to win. As had happened to Jason in his dream, it was not uncommon for drivers to black out taking the Elbow, allowing their desire to win to overcome their good sense.

There was also one extra feature, unique to this race, known as *the Fifteen-Second Rule*.

In short, every racer had to stay within fifteen seconds of the lead car. As the leader passed underneath each bridge, a timer was initiated. After fifteen seconds, the ion waterfall on that bridge flicked from gold to red—and the gap in the waterfall closed, turning it into an impassable wall of ions. Meaning that if you failed to stay within fifteen seconds of the leader, you could physically go no farther. You were out of the race.

At this point in the Masters, since there were only eight contenders left, the scoring system also changed.

For the final two races, the winner still got ten points.

The second placed racer, however, now only got eight points; third got six points; fourth: four points; fifth: two points; and the last three drivers, nothing. Those racers who DNF'd—Did Not Finish—still got a flat zero points.

For Jason, the situation was clear.

Sitting on only eight points, a full eight points behind the leaders in the series, he needed a good finish in this race—top two at least—and he needed some of the other racers to finish poorly or not at all.

But if he'd learned anything this year, it was that in hover car racing, *anything could happen*.

As daylight broke on Saturday, Manhattan Island had essentially become one gigantic stadium.

Enormous crowds swarmed all over the outer banks of the East River, the Harlem River, and the Hudson River, all facing inward. While on Manhattan itself, New

Yorkers had commandeered every piece of available viewing space—from parks and buildings to the major freeways that ringed the edges of the island: the Henry Hudson Parkway, West Street, and the FDR—all looking outward.

And the subject of their collective gaze:

The eight humming rocket cars hovering above the waves of the East River, in the shadow of the mighty Brooklyn Bridge.

Jason and the Bug sat hunched in the *Argonaut*, eyeing the river stretching away before them.

Fabian's *Marseilles Falcon* sat on their left and Trouveau's *Vizir*—Jason had discovered that it was named after Napoleon's horse—on their right.

"Anything can happen . . . ," Jason said aloud.

It was about to.

The lights went green and the race began.

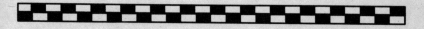

Eight cars.

120 laps.

On one very short track.

To Jason, the three rivers of New York resembled one continuous watery trench, flanked by hills of roaring spectators and spanned intermittently by sweeping bridges, from which cascaded the spectacular golden ion waterfalls.

The first bridge after the Brooklyn was the Manhattan Bridge, but since it was so close to the Brooklyn, its waterfall wasn't initiated till Lap 2. But the next bridge, the colossal Williamsburg Bridge, like the first turn of any race, was a crunch point.

Its golden waterfall was most certainly active—and by the time the eight racers reached it, they had to be in single file in order to pass through the narrow opening in its curtain of golden ions.

The surface of the East River rushed under the nose of the *Argonaut* as Jason threw every lever forward, banking with the leftward bend in the river toward the tiny gap under the Williamsburg Bridge.

He saw the bridge, saw the gap, saw all the speeding cars around him and wondered: *How the hell are we all going to fit through?*

But in the moment before the bridge was upon them, all eight cars converged like the teeth of a zipper and roared— *shoom-shoom-shoom-shoom*—through the narrow gap.

But then as he shot through the gap in the waterfall in the middle of the field, Jason saw that one car hadn't quite made it through, and had instead shot right through the ion cascade.

It was the second U.S. Air Force driver, Dwayne Lewicki, in his modified F-55 fighter, Car No.23.

Trailing two cars behind Jason, Lewicki's car emerged on the other side of the waterfall, seemingly all right—but it wasn't.

It was completely without power.

Slowly, painfully, inexorably, the car peeled away to the right in a soaring downward arc, before it came to an abrupt jarring halt in a dead zone in front of the spectators on the eastern shore—out of the race.

"Game on," Jason said.

Jason roared around the track—all but overwhelmed by the intensity of the racing.

This was unlike anything he'd experienced at Race School. Cars whizzed across his nose at reckless speeds. Racers bumped and pushed each other. And the crowd, it was always there, always around him, roaring, cheering, almost . . . well . . . *baying* for blood. It kind of felt like an old Roman chariot race.

The two Renault drivers, Fabian and Trouveau, had obviously decided to make Jason's life hell. All around the first lap—and then the second and the third—the two Frenchmen badgered Jason, the pair of them taking calculated swipes at both his tailfin and his nose, zeroing in on the *Argonaut* with their bladed nosewings.

Every time they cut in, the New York crowds booed.

And every time Jason evaded their thrusts, the crowds cheered. He held them off doggedly.

But it was only a matter of time till their attacks did some damage, and on Lap 6 they did.

At Liberty's Elbow, the two French cars cut across the bow of the *Argonaut* in such a way that Jason either pulled out of the turn or lost his nosewing.

He pulled out of the turn—

—and decelerated—

—and watched as the field raced away from him.

"Darn it!" he yelled. "French jerks!"

He gunned the *Argonaut* once more, and shot off in pursuit—now chasing the fifteen-second rule.

At each bridge now, he saw a giant digital countdown, telling him how far ahead the leader was (of course, it was Alessandro Romba).

Jason hit the Start-Finish Line at the Brooklyn Bridge eleven seconds behind Romba. Close. But okay.

But in a race like this—by its very nature, tight and close—that kind of lead could only be regathered in the pits or with the help of a crash.

In the end, Jason would benefit from both.

Pit stops in a collective pursuit race were preset—so as not to allow cheap knockouts when someone pitted. In this race, they were preset to take place every twenty laps.

At those stops, Sally performed like a genius. And it was she who hauled in Alessandro Romba's lead—in stops on Laps 20, 40, 60, and 80, in one of those stops, hauling in three whole seconds.

And then things started to get interesting.

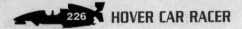

LAP: 105 OF 120

Romba was still in the lead, in his silver and black Lockheed-Martin.

The USAF pilot, Carver, was in second place in his military-blue F-55.

Then there was a pack of four—among them, Jason.

Last of all, in seventh place, came Jason's quasi-teammate in the Lombardi Racing Team, Pablo Riviera.

Riviera was languishing in last place, having woefully botched a pit stop on Lap 100, and was now traveling along only just inside the fifteen-second mark.

And so, in a moment of desperate insanity, he took on the second meat grinder—since it afforded the single greatest gain on the course. It could turn a thirteen-second deficit into a three-second one.

He didn't know—or perhaps he didn't have the skill or the nerve to know—that in order to overcome the meat grinders of New York, you had to take them at absolutely full speed: 510 mph.

And entering a tight iron tunnel no bigger than a garage door at close to the speed of sound is even harder than it sounds.

Riviera shot into the meat grinder at a cool 470 mph.

The long dark cylindrical tunnel enveloped him.

And then the tunnel around him began to iris shut, its gigantic iron cleaves squeezing inward with a loud mechanical clanking, like a giant industrial python swallowing its prey.

And in a moment of clarity, Riviera realized he wasn't going to make it.

He screamed.

The meat grinder squealed with rust as it closed around him.

Its shrieking walls sheared off the tips of his wings first . . . then they crushed his side air intakes . . . and his tailfin . . . and . . .

The crumpled remains of Riviera's F-3000 were spat out the other end of the meat grinder, battered and unrecognizable; it tumbled into the river, the only thing that

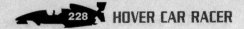

had survived: the driver's reinforced safety cockpit. Riviera was alive—just—and only because of the super-solid construction of his car (and the fact that the meat grinder didn't squeeze all the way inward). Not in any way because of his own skill.

Now only six drivers remained in the race.

Two separate battles were now taking place on every lap.

Romba and Carver for the lead.

Jason and the two Renault drivers for third. And trailing behind them, just managing to keep inside the fifteen-second rule, the General Motors factory team driver, an older Australian driver named Mark Skaife in car 102.

In fact, the fifteen-second rule performed an admirable service: It kept all of them bunched close together—within striking distance—so that when the chance came, every driver was in a position to strike.

Then the chance came.

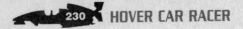

When two things happened at once:

First, Angus Carver tried to overtake Alessandro Romba as they roared up the side of Ward's-Randall's Island on Lap 110. Carver tried to sneak inside Romba, but Romba held his line stubbornly, and as they hit the left-hander at the top of the island, they collided—badly—and separated, lurching wildly in either direction, *both of them* hitting the nearby demag lights.

The other thing that happened (at the exact same time) was this: As they shot up the East River behind the two leaders, Fabian and Trouveau, working together, boxed Jason in on the left-hand side of the track, so that when they hit Ward's-Randall's Island, Jason had only two options: crash into Ward's Island, or go left—toward the second meat grinder.

Jason went left.

And he accelerated.

Gave it everything he had. He'd seen the meat

grinders enough on TV over the years, and every year the commentators said the same thing: You couldn't beat them at anything less than top speed.

So he hit the gas and rushed round the base of Ward's-Randall's Island and beheld the entry to the second meat grinder.

It looked tiny.

Really tiny.

This would be like firing a bullet into a keyhole.

The *Argonaut* rushed toward the tiny opening. Its speedometer topped 500 mph . . .

505 mph . . . then 510 mph before—

VOOOOOOM!

The *Argonaut* blasted into the tight cylindrical tunnel— and immediately the tunnel began to iris inward.

Jason leaned forward in his seat.

The Bug looked up at the rapidly "collapsing" tunnel all around them.

Then the irising walls were so close, they started sparking against the *Argonaut*'s wingtips, and Jason thought

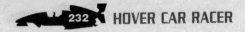

his car was almost certainly going to die when—
whoosh—they blasted out into dazzling sunshine again
and found themselves . . .

. . . in the lead.

With only ten laps to go.

The Bug exclaimed something.

Jason smiled. "I'm telling Mom you swore."

But the jackals weren't far behind.

Because of their collision, Romba and Carver were
toast, and they were quickly swamped by Trouveau and
then Fabian and then Skaife. (Romba and Carver would
ultimately duke it out for the still-important two points
available to the fifth-place racer, fighting right up until
they were both eliminated by the fifteen-second rule—in
the end, Romba outlasted Carver.)

Meanwhile, up front, it was Jason against the rest—
and with ten laps to run, he now had a golden
opportunity *to win the race*!

And from that moment, with adrenaline coursing

through his entire body, Jason flew nine of the best laps of his life.

The two Frenchmen couldn't believe that he'd come out the other side of the meat grinder. They charged with a vengeance.

It was Trouveau—needing the points more than Fabian—who charged harder, and when he stormed through the first meat grinder on Lap 115, he was suddenly hammering on Jason's tail.

The last four laps of the race would be four of the toughest Jason had ever experienced.

Trouveau hounded him.

But Jason took every turn perfectly.

Well, almost every turn. On each lap, Trouveau gained on him at Liberty's Elbow. The French driver seemed to know it was Jason's weak point—it was as if he could *smell* Jason's fear. He knew that Jason took it gingerly, frightened of the G-forces, frightened of blacking out.

And as they commenced the last lap of the race—Lap

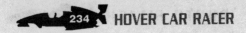

120 of 120—Trouveau was traveling almost alongside the *Argonaut*.

And deep in his heart of hearts, Jason knew what Trouveau was going to do.

Trouveau was going to take him at the Elbow.

Up the East River, following the safe route now. Into the narrower Harlem River, under all the bridges spanning it— before blasting out into the Hudson, down its long wide straight, hitting top speed, before suddenly, *she* came into view.

Lady Liberty.

Jason saw her and grimaced.

He knew the score—the Bug had done the math after Romba and Carver had been eliminated: An eight-point second-place finish wouldn't be enough to beat Carver in the overall standings. To go through to the next race, Jason needed the full ten points. He needed to win.

Death or glory, he thought.

And as he hit the Elbow, he knew which one he'd choose.

• • •

Into the Elbow, banking left, their cars almost vertical, flying hard.

And then Trouveau—as expected—made his move.

But this time Jason held his line.

And Trouveau was a little shocked.

Halfway round the Elbow—

—and Jason's vision began to blur at the edges.

7-Gs . . .

Further round the enormous hairpin . . . and his vision began to *darken*.

I can make this . . . , he told himself.

I can make this . . .

8-Gs . . .

Blinking. Trying . . . so hard . . .

8.5 . . .

. . . to . . . stay . . . conscious . . .

Trouveau was almost beside him now, but the Frenchman couldn't get past.

9-Gs . . .

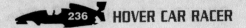

And Jason's face was pressed against his skull, his cheeks sucking backward, his teeth clenched hard, and he realized with a thrill that this time—yes!—he was going to make it. . . .

Then he blacked out.

Jason awoke—

—to the sound of ecstatically cheering crowds . . . and to someone banging on his helmet.

It was the Bug hammering on his helmet, trying to rouse him.

As for the crowd, they seemed to be cheering: "We love the Buuuuug! We love the Buuuuug!"

Jason was sitting in the *Argonaut*, but it was stationary now—caught in a dead zone—hovering above the low waves of the East River, but *past the Finish Line*.

Jason looked about himself in astonishment—he had

no recollection of how he had got from Liberty's Elbow to the Finish Line.

Then he saw an action replay on a giant-screen TV on the riverbank: saw the *Argonaut* blast out of the Elbow, leveling out of its high-banking turn ahead of the *Vizir*, and roar past the camera.

And there, depicted in glorious slow-motion on the television image, leaning over Jason from behind, clutching at the *Argonaut*'s steering wheel, guiding the car over the last few hundred yards, was the one student at the International Race School who had survived a 9-G banking turn.

The Bug.

More than that, the *Argonaut* had retained its speed from the turn (evidently, despite losing consciousness, Jason had kept leaning on his thrusters), and with the Bug at the controls, it had outrun Trouveau to the Brooklyn Bridge!

The *Argonaut,* with its pilot unconscious and its navigator leaning over him to steer, had won the darn race!

Action replay

Now the Bug was smiling broadly. He explained to Jason what had happened.

"I what?" Jason asked. "I kept all our thrusters on, even after I knocked myself out?"

The Bug nodded, added something.

"You could say that," Jason replied. "You could say I wanted to win this race *really* badly."

The points immediately went up on the scoreboard.

Ten points for Jason.

Eight for Trouveau.

Six for Fabian, who took third place easily.

Four for the Australian Skaife—a fine effort, but not enough to take him to the final round.

And a most unusual two points for Alessandro Romba, for his fifth-place finish; while the USAF pilot, Carver, got zero for coming in sixth.

And suddenly, with the two USAF pilots both scoring no points at all and the overall leader scoring poorly, the scoreboard told a new tale:

DRIVER	LIBERTY SUPERSPRINT	MANHATTAN GATE RACE	THE PURSUIT	THE QUEST	TOTAL
1. ROMBA, A. (1) *Lockheed-Martin Racing*	10	6	2		18
2. FABIAN (17) *Team Renault*	9	7	6		22
3. TROUVEAU, E. (40) *Team Renault*	8	3	8		19
4. CARVER, A. (24) *USAF Racing*	7	10	0		17
5. LEWICKI, D .(23) *USAF Racing*	6	9	DNF		15
6. SKAIFE, M. (102) *General Motors Factory Team*	5	4	4		13
7. HASSAN, R. (2) *Lockheed-Martin Racing*	4	0			4
8. REIN, D. (45) *Boeing-Ford Team*	3	1			4
9. CHOW, A. (38) *China State Racing*	2	DNF			2
10. REITZE, R. (51) *Porsche Racing*	1	2			3
11. RIVIERA, P. (12) *Lombardi Racing Team*	0	5	DNF		5
12. CHASER, J. (55) *Lombardi Racing Team*	0	8	10		18

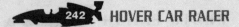

DRIVER	LIBERTY SUPERSPRINT	MANHATTAN GATE RACE	THE PURSUIT	THE QUEST	TOTAL
13. REITZE, H. (50) Porsche Racing	DNF				
14. MARTINEZ, C. (44) Boeing-Ford Team	DNF				
15. PETERS, B. (05) General Motors Factory Team	DNF				
16. IDEKI, K. (11) Yamaha Racing Team	DNF				

All of a sudden, Angus Carver had gone from leading with seventeen points, to being eliminated with seventeen points, while Fabian—wily Fabian—had shot up the scoreboard with his solid six-point finish, surging into first place with twenty-two points, three points clear of his nearest rival, his team-mate, Etienne Trouveau.

But most astonishing of all was Jason, who, with his massive ten-point bonanza, found himself with eighteen points, and in the top four, leapfrogging three racers with one big jump. The Bug had been right: That final turn had made all the difference; eight points would not have been enough.

Jason couldn't believe it.

His parents couldn't believe it.

The crowds couldn't believe it.

The commentators couldn't believe it.

Thanks to the Bug, the one and only Bug, the *Argonaut* was in the fourth and final race of the New York Masters.

NEW YORK CITY, USA (SATURDAY EVENING)

That evening, a silence fell on the New Jersey home of Jason's cousins.

After Team *Argonaut*'s efforts in the Pursuit earlier that day, one would have expected an uproarious celebration, with champagne corks popping and soft drink spraying.

But no, that wasn't happening tonight.

The weight of it all had finally hit home: the magnitude of what Team *Argonaut* had achieved this week. After three ultratough pro-level races, tomorrow Jason, the Bug, and Sally would be participating in one of the most prestigious events in world racing—and also one of the most dangerous.

Everyone sat around the dinner table in contemplative

silence: Jason, the Bug, Henry and Martha Chaser, the Chaser cousins, Sally McDuff and her family, and Ariel Piper.

Indeed, the silence—a grim hush of fear and awe—was deafening.

The only one who wasn't fazed by it all was Scott Syracuse, but then, he'd been here before in a professional capacity and so was used to the pressure.

"You know . . . ," Syracuse said, breaking the uncomfortable silence, "the other racers, they're only men."

Others in the room kept their heads bowed. Jason alone looked up at his teacher.

Syracuse shrugged. "People see racers like Fabian and Romba, and they think they're superhuman. Men of steel. Bold champions who fly at astronomical speeds without fear or nerves. But they're not superheroes. Oh no, they're not. They are ordinary men, with fears and loves and weaknesses like you and me.

"This is why we love sportspeople—from Tiger Woods to Donald Bradman to Muhammad Ali—they handle a kind of pressure that most people cannot even imagine. They stand on a golf course or in a stadium or in a ring, with hundreds of thousands of viewers watching them, and somehow their legs don't fall out from under them. And then—*then*—they *keep* standing and, under all that scrutiny, *they do what they have practiced for so long and they do it well*. That's why we love them. We think *we* would fail, and yet they don't. But that doesn't mean they aren't afraid.

"Jason, Bug, Sally. As your teacher, I've watched you develop this past year; watched you grow from young, wide-eyed hopefuls with some talent . . . into *racers*. When you started with me, you were good. Now you are great. Great at your individual duties, and a great team—from going to lessons when you were too tired to think; to pitching in together to perform manual pit stops; to pushing your car over the line; to the Bug taking over the steering when it was necessary.

"You're *racers* now. And believe me, you're ready for this. You may not think so, but as someone who knows racing, trust my judgment: You are ready to stand up in front of the world, and your legs will not fall out from under you. You've done the work, you have the skill, and you most certainly have the desire. It's time for you to do what you came here to do: Win the Masters."

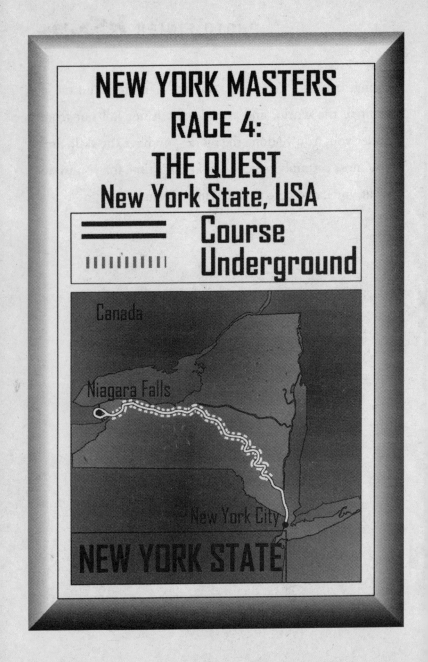

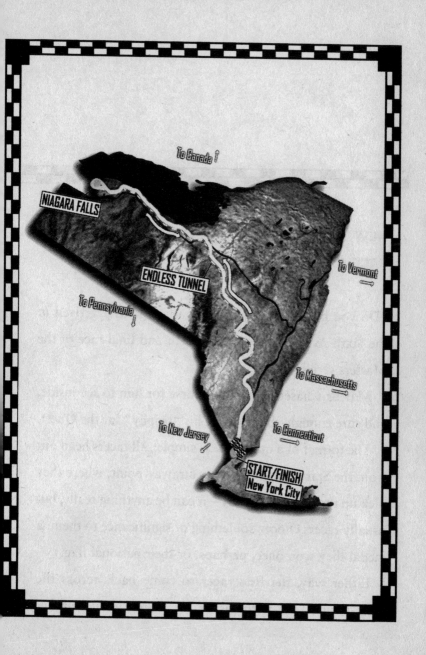

To Canada ↑

NIAGARA FALLS

ENDLESS TUNNEL

To Vermont →

To Pennsylvania ↓

To Massachusetts →

To New Jersey ↙

To Connecticut →

START/FINISH
New York City

NEW YORK CITY, USA (SUNDAY)
RACE 4: THE QUEST

"Do you have it, Mom?" Jason asked as they arrived in the Sixth Avenue pits for the fourth and final race of the Masters series.

Martha Chaser opened her purse for him to see inside, and sure enough, there it was, his "trophy" for the Quest.

The format of a quest race is simple: All racers head out from the Start-Finish Line to a faraway point, where they pick up their chosen trophy—it can be anything really, but usually racers choose something of significance to them: a medal they won once, perhaps, or their national flag.

Either way, the first racer to come back across the Start-Finish Line *with his or her trophy in his or her possession* wins. The twist comes in the journey itself—and the journey in the Masters' Quest is a particularly difficult one.

Typically, Jason's mother had fashioned a very appropriate trophy for Team *Argonaut* to use in Race 4.

"I think we have to give it to one of the officials," Jason said, taking it from her.

As they reached their pit bay, he handed it to the race official who would transport all four racers' trophies to the farthest point of the Quest course.

The *Argonaut* sat in its pit bay, glistening, shining, *waiting*. It was as if the little blue, white, and silver car were alive, energized, ready to go, stamping its hoofs in anticipation of the challenge ahead of it today.

Jason eyed his car with pride, thinking of all they had been through together—from the Regional Champion-ships in the swamps of Carpentaria, to his epic efforts at Race School: the grueling tournament, taking on the Clashing Bergs in the final race; and now, his feats here in New York.

He patted the *Argonaut*'s left wing.

"Well, car," he said, "here we are again. One more race, that's all I ask of you. One more race. Let's do it."

And with a final pat, he strode away from the car to go and get suited up for the race.

He never saw the tiny explosive device—it was the size of a pinhead—attached to the tailfin of his beloved *Argonaut*.

It had been placed there during the night by a light-fingered hand . . . a hand that had paid off one of the security guards to gain access to the pit area . . . a hand that had laid a similar device on another *Argonaut* once before.

The four cars sat on Fifth Avenue, all aimed northward.

Alessandro Romba—in his silver and black Lockheed-Martin.

Fabian and Etienne Trouveau—in their purple and gold Renaults.

And Jason—in the *Argonaut*.

This is what it came down to.

Four contenders.

All within four points of each other.

Romba, Trouveau, and Jason had to win Race 4—and

have some other placings go their way—in order to take the Masters.

Fabian, however—three points clear of his nearest rival—could come second, garnering eight points, and still take the overall title.

The course for the Quest was a long and arduous one—taking the racers all the way across New York State, right to Niagara Falls on the U.S.-Canadian border. There the racers would collect their trophies from a platform suspended high above the falls and begin the journey back to Manhattan.

Now, while the journey both ways was extraordinarily difficult, it was also astonishingly beautiful, but in an unusual way.

For the main feature of the course was a superlong underground highway known as the Endless Tunnel. Before the invention of hover cars, the U.S. government had started construction of an underground super-highway designed to go from the Canadian border all the way down to Florida, to be known as Superhighway 2.

But then along came hover cars and the project was abandoned, and only the section through New York State was completed—and even then, only roughly.

What remained was a rough-hewn network of long octagonal tunnels cutting through all sorts of underground environments—old mines, subterranean chasms, rivers, and waterfalls. Indeed, the construction of the highway had led to the discovery of the now-famous Twin Caves, the largest underground caverns in the world.

Naturally, the Endless Tunnel was now equipped with many small ion waterfalls that cut the tunnel's width in half. Plus lots of single-file-only bridges over the underground gorges and rivers, and not a few dead-end forks: Navigators were provided with a map of the tunnel, and their role in the race was crucial.

Jason sat in his cockpit, eyeing the skyscraper-and-grandstand-lined canyon of Fifth Avenue stretching away before him.

"Your legs will not fall from under you," he said aloud.

The Bug didn't hear him properly, and asked what he'd said.

"Nothing, little brother. Nothing."

The crowd murmured—would Alessandro Romba win this race and take the Grand Slam? Or the two Frenchmen? Or perhaps even the young outsider, Jason?

Jason's parents watched from the grandstand nearest to the Start-Finish Line. Sitting with them were Umberto Lombardi, Scott Syracuse, the McDuff clan, and Ariel Piper. Henry Chaser was literally on the edge of his seat with excitement.

Then suddenly a loud electronic tone warned everyone that the start lights would ignite in three seconds.

Red light—

Yellow light—

Green light—

Go!

The world blurred.

Superspeed. And Jason found himself pushing the *Argonaut* to new limits.

Skyscrapers became bridges then houses then open highway as the racers shot up Interstate 87, charging northward, with every piece of available land covered with spectators.

Then the landscape quickly became tree-covered hills, bridges, and rivers, and—all too soon—the Catskill Mountains came into view. And waiting for him at their base, Jason knew, was the entrance to the famed and feared Endless Tunnel.

Romba was in the lead, where he liked to be, while Jason and the two Renaults jockeyed for second place, overtaking each other regularly—and all the while, the two French drivers flashed their razor-sharp nosewings dangerously close to Jason's flanks.

And then Jason beheld the entrance to the tunnel.

It was a massive gray concrete arch, solid as hell, with a dark passageway behind it that yawned black. The opening was flanked by a sea of cheering spectators.

Shoom!

Jason rushed into the blackness.

• • •

Arched concrete pillars whistled by overhead in a dizzying display of hyper-repetition. Actually, they weren't so much pillars as "ribs"—the ribs of the octagonal tunnel.

The four cars roared like rockets through the winding passageway, banking with the bends, flattening out with the straightaways.

Romba—Jason—Fabian—Trouveau.

At certain points, ion waterfalls halved the width of the Tunnel, and they had to form up into single file to get past the glittering golden curtains—and sometimes weave left and right when a second or a third ion waterfall appeared directly after the previous one, but on the other side of the underground passage.

And then, gloriously, Jason burst out onto a superlong natural bridge that spanned a subterranean gorge. Bottomless black raced by on either side of the fenceless bridge. But before he could gaze in wonder at the spectacular scenery, Jason was plunged into claustrophobic tunnel territory once again.

Forks began to appear in the tunnel system.

And for a time everyone just followed Alessandro Romba—trusting his navigator's map-reading skills—but then Romba got ahead of the others and suddenly the Bug had to make the *Argonaut*'s navigation calls.

But not for long.

Fabian—eager to stay in second place and thus ensure that he won the Masters—started harrying Jason with the help of Trouveau.

The *Argonaut* sped round a bend, avoiding an ion waterfall, before—*whoosh*—it blasted out into an absolutely enormous cavern, the first of the Twin Caves, known as the Small Cave.

Stunning waterfalls cascaded from fissures in the side of the immense cavern, falling 700 feet down a multi-tiered rock wall before disappearing into darkness. Temporary underground hover stands filled with spectators lined the cavern, their chants echoing in the massive space.

A wide bending S-shaped bridge snaked its way across

the face of the multistreamed falls—at some points dip-
ping behind the curtains of rushing water. The hover cars
on the bridge were dwarfed by the sheer size of the underground water system.

It was here that the two Renaults tried to finish Jason
off for good.

The bending bridge was wide enough for the three of
them, but it narrowed to a two-car-wide tunnel at its
end.

Ominously, the two Renaults swept up on either side of
the *Argonaut*.

Jason snapped left, then right. Saw Fabian at his left,
Trouveau on his right—both of them so close that he
could almost touch them.

A Renault sandwich.

"Uh-oh . . . ," Jason said.

The Renaults had him exactly where they wanted
him—in a technique they'd used so many times before to
nail their rivals. All Fabian had to do now was push Jason
onto Trouveau's bladed nosewing.

Fabian started ramming Jason, forcing him right, forcing him toward . . .

. . . Trouveau's flashing nosewing.

Jason rammed Fabian back, fighting the push—nervously eyeing the rapidly approaching tunnel entrance ahead.

Then Trouveau also pulled in close, bringing his fearsome silver nosewing to within inches of the *Argonaut*'s.

Jason swung his head left and right. There was nowhere to go. He was being run onto Trouveau's blades and there was nothing he could do about it.

Any second now, they would have him. . . .

Any second . . .

Fabian gave him a final push.

Got him.

RACE 4: THE QUEST
SECTION: THE ENDLESS TUNNEL (OUTBOUND)

But as Fabian made the killing blow, Jason did something totally unexpected.

He slammed on his brakes.

The *Argonaut* slid backward in the air, and the result of this sudden action was as spectacular as it was surprising.

Fabian—previously pushing hard against the *Argonaut*—suddenly found himself pushing against nothing at all, so his car lunged forward in the air. Before he could do anything about it, Fabian saw his own bladed nosewing shear right through Trouveau's!

Trouveau's eyes bulged as he saw his nosewing drop away—at which point he lost all control of his vehicle and the *Vizir* veered to the right, speeding perilously close to the edge of the winding bridge and the deep drop below it, before it smashed with terrible force into the vertical concrete frame of the tunnel entrance at the end of the gigantic cave.

Car hit stone.

At 440 mph.

In a single instant, the *Vizir* transformed from hover car to fireball.

The explosion rang out in the cavern—and the crowds in the stands rose in horror. Trouveau and his navigator would ultimately walk away from the crash, dazed and dizzy, saved only by their reinforced cockpit and anticrash features. The *Vizir*, on the other hand, would never race again.

It was left splayed across the right-hand side of the tunnel entrance, blocking half the way.

As for Jason, he was still rocketing along at speed—his braking maneuver had only been brief, so he hadn't lost that much ground on Fabian—and the two of them shot past the wreckage of the *Vizir* in single file and disappeared into the two-car-wide tunnel at the end of the Small Cave.

The tunnel that led out from the Small Cave bent in a wide, wide curve to the right—testing each driver's G-force-resistance like Liberty's Elbow did—before it opened onto the second of the Twin Caves.

This was the Big Cave.

And it made the Small Cave look puny.

It was the largest natural underground space in the world, discovered only a few years previously, and it was utterly breathtaking. Towering waterfalls and rocky pinnacles as high as skyscrapers lined the superlong cavern. Magnificent, naturally formed aqueducts connected some of the pinnacles, and the water running down them spilled off their ends, spraying into the air before dropping away into darkness.

A gently sloping bridge of rock ran all the way down the length of the mighty cave, stabbed here and there by thin vertical waterfalls that over many years had cut clean through its edges, and it was along this that the racers sped, winding between the thin but powerful jet streams of water.

Romba, then Fabian, then Jason.

To the roars of the crowds in the hover stands, the three remaining racers blasted down the rockway and disappeared into the final section of the Endless Tunnel—a section that ended at Niagara.

Niagara Falls.

The sight, glorious. The sound, deafening. The crowds flanking the world's most famous outdoor falls: massing and roiling and bursting with anticipation.

All eyes were glued to the tiny pipelike tunnel that poked out from the base of the main falls, waiting to see which racer would emerge first.

Alessandro Romba did.

And the crowds went nuts.

Fabian blasted out next, followed last of all by Jason.

Niagara Falls

The three cars banked quickly, sweeping up the hill on the U.S. side of the Falls, before they all stopped at the landward end of a long thin rail-less footbridge that extended out over the flowing river, at the very precipice of the Falls.

Jason leaped out of the *Argonaut* and, chasing Romba and Fabian *on foot*, he dashed out across the long narrow bridge.

Sitting on a platform at the end of the footbridge were four podiums, and on each podium sat each racer's trophy.

Romba's trophy was the Italian flag. He snatched it and turned and began the run back to his car . . . and the return journey home.

Fabian's trophy was typically Fabian: It was a framed picture of himself standing with the *Marseilles Falcon*. He grabbed it and dashed back to his car, pushing roughly past Jason as they ran past each other on the narrow bridge.

Last of all, Jason came to his podium.

And he beheld his trophy, crafted by his mother.

It shone in the sunlight like a treasure, haloed by the rainbow created by the spray of the Falls.

A small piece of soft wool.

Painted all in gold.

A golden fleece.

Like his classical namesake, Jason grabbed the fleece, turned, and then ran as fast as he could back to his chariot, and thus began the most thrilling hour of racing he had ever experienced in his short life.

RACE 4: THE QUEST
SECTION: THE ENDLESS TUNNEL (INBOUND)

Jason jumped into the driver's seat of the *Argonaut* and hit the gas.

The little Ferrari roared off the mark, swinging in a wide circle in the turnaround at the top of Niagara Falls, before descending down the roadway to the base of the Falls, where it swung out over the river and shot like a bullet back into the Endless Tunnel.

Into the dark again.

Heading for home.

Roaring, charging, chasing, racing.

Jason hammered the *Argonaut* through the branchlike passageways of the Endless Tunnel, ducking left, veering right, now engaged with Romba and Fabian in a headlong race for home.

He saw Fabian's taillights glowing red not far ahead of him—and suddenly there came a voice in Jason's helmet earpiece, a French-accented voice that shouldn't have been there.

"You cannot win, boy."

It was Fabian.

He must have discovered Jason's radio frequency and now, in the crunch zone of the race, decided to put in a taunting call. This was highly improper, but not technically illegal.

"Why keep trying?" Fabian said. *"You've done so well for a child. Why not leave the rest of this race to the men?"*

Jason eyed the Frenchman's taillights.

"I'm coming after you, Fabian," he said firmly.

And he was.

He was gaining steadily on Fabian as they shot through the dark rocky tunnels, so much so that when they hit the

Big Cave, the *Argonaut* sprang alongside the *Marseilles Falcon* on its right-hand side.

Fabian saw Jason and frowned—

"Peek-a-boo," Jason said.

In reply Fabian rammed him.

But Jason swung wide, softening the blow.

This only seemed to enrage Fabian even more, and as they shot up the long ramp of the Big Cave, Fabian slammed the *Marseilles Falcon* into the *Argonaut* again.

Jason, however, was up to the challenge, and he held his line as the two cars swooped up the bridge side by side and shot into the long sweeping (now) leftward-curving tunnel that connected the Big Cave to the Small Cave.

Banking with the turn.

Flying hard.

Flying fast.

Fabian on the inside, Jason on the outside, their cars positively galloping, tearing the very fabric of the air with their speed.

And then, in a fleeting moment, Jason saw Fabian's

eyes in his helmet—saw them glaring over at Jason with pure derision and hatred.

"*I'm gonna get you, you little punk!*"

"Not today," Jason said.

"*And why exactly not?*"

"Because I've remembered something you haven't," Jason said.

And as he said it, they rounded the final segment of the curve together, perfectly side by side—Fabian on the left, Jason on the right—and the thing that Jason had remembered suddenly came upon them.

The wreckage of Etienne Trouveau's car.

It was still crumpled up against the entrance to this tunnel—now the exit—blocking the entire left-hand side of the track.

Fabian's side of the track.

Fabian saw it too late, and his eyes boggled at the sight—and at the realization that Jason had got the better of him; had deliberately gotten him to travel on this side of the track, heading straight for his teammate's wreck.

Fabian screamed.

Then he covered his head as the *Marseilles Falcon* exploded *clean through* the remains of the *Vizir*, sending pieces of the two Renaults showering out in a huge star-shaped spray—while at the same time, the *Argonaut* shot past the double wreck in total safety.

The central core of Fabian's car actually survived the trip through the *Vizir*—although unfortunately for Fabian, its wings, nosewing, and tailfin didn't.

The battered remains of his car shot off the nearest edge of the S-shaped bridge in the Small Cave and sailed down into blackness . . .

. . . where, perhaps undeservedly, it would be caught in a safety dead zone, its race run.

Needless to say, the crash's effect on the race, on the entire Masters Series, was electrifying.

Fabian had just DNF'd—meaning he would get *no* points at all for this race. His Masters Series was over.

Now the Masters would be fought out by the last two

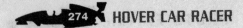

racers on the track: Alessandro Romba and Jason Chaser.

With the two Renaults out of his hair for good and flying on outrageous amounts of adrenaline, Jason now eyed the taillights of Alessandro Romba.

La Bomba Romba.

The No. 1–ranked driver in the world, the man seeking to become the first racer ever to claim the Grand Slam, the man who this whole year had never been cleanly passed.

Until today, Jason thought.

A two-horse race.

Romba fleeing.

Jason chasing.

Chasing him as hard as he could.

Down the length of the Small Cave, then into the labyrinthine passages of the tunnel.

Romba drove hard.

Jason drove perfectly.

And over the course of twenty minutes, he *gained* on

the World No. 1, moving within a car-length of him before—

—sunlight assaulted them both as they blasted together out of the tunnel.

Onto the interstate now, sweeping left and right between the trees and hills—with Jason hammering on Romba's tail, giving the World No.1 absolute hell.

Then Jason made his move, tried to get past Romba on the inside left.

Romba blocked the move—legally, fluidly.

Jason tried again, this time on the right.

And Romba blocked him again.

Jason persisted, left, then right, searching doggedly for a gap, showing the World No.1 no respect.

Then again Jason went left—and Romba went that way too—but this time it was a perfectly disguised fake and Jason suddenly cut right . . .

. . . and zipped past Alessandro Romba as Romba overbalanced to the left!

The crowds lining the highway gasped.

Then they *roared* with joy, delighted at Jason's skill.

It wasn't a crash or luck or some foul move that had got Jason past Romba.

It had just been darn good driving.

And suddenly, with only ten minutes left in the New York Masters, *Jason found himself in the lead.*

New York City rose in the distance.

Whizzing down the interstate, Jason saw its high skyscrapers stabbing the sky.

He gunned the *Argonaut*, trying to shut out all thought of being *in the lead*, being *out in front*, being on the cusp of achieving everything he had ever dreamed of.

Don't think about winning! he told himself. *Don't jump the gun!*

Win the race first.

So he concentrated with all his might.

And in the final runup to Manhattan, he actually extended his lead on Romba, moving at first a car-length, then a few lengths ahead of the Italian.

Then it was over the Broadway Bridge at the top of Manhattan Island, and suddenly he was back in the city and its maze of hard right-angled corners.

The assembled crowds roared at his every turn.

Romba was now 200 feet behind him.

And as he swung out onto Fifth Avenue and realized that he had no more turns to take—that this was the end—that he'd done it—Jason allowed himself a half-grin.

He'd done it. . . .

And then a figure in the crowd watching Jason shoot down Fifth Avenue toward the Finish Line pressed a button on a remote control, triggering the pinhead-size explosive device attached to the tailfin of the *Argonaut*.

For the second time that year—and for the second time in a Grand Slam Race—the *Argonaut*'s tailfin spontaneously exploded.

No! Jason thought. *Not on the home straightaway!*

"Hang on, Bug!" was all he had time to yell.

Its tailfin gone, the speeding *Argonaut* dropped its nose instantly and ploughed at a sizzling 500 mph into the pavement of Fifth Avenue.

Sparks flew everywhere.

The *Argonaut*'s nosewing dislodged immediately and flew away, loose pieces of the car were stripped off by the wind, while its wings bounced against the pavement and were torn clean off.

And the battered little *Argonaut* skidded to a sideways halt in the middle of Fifth Avenue, a tantalizing five hundred feet short of the Finish Line, before it tipped clumsily onto its side, its cockpit pointed toward the line.

Jason snapped his neck upwards and saw—tilted sideways—the Finish Line, so close but so far away.

"Bug! You okay?"

The Bug said he was.

In a flash, Jason assessed his options.

He knew Romba was close behind him—and by the sound of it, almost on him—too close to beat to the line on foot as the Bug had done to Barnaby back at Race School.

"Darn it!" he yelled. "I am *not* gonna lose this race!"

And as he felt Romba's car come up beside his stationary position, inspiration struck and Jason jammed his golden fleece in his lap, unclipped his transponder-equipped steering wheel, and did the only thing he could think to do to win the race.

He yanked on his ejection lever.

RACE 4: THE QUEST
SECTION: FIFTH AVENUE (INBOUND)

It was an image no racegoer would ever forget.

The black Lockheed of Alessandro Romba sweeping past the crumpled wreck of the *Argonaut* just as—*shoooooom!*—Jason, on his ejection seat, came shooting out of the wreck, rocketing horizontally and headfirst, like a human cannonball, a bare two feet above the surface of Fifth Avenue where he . . .

. . . *overtook* Romba's car in flight . . .

. . . and shot over the Finish Line one single foot ahead of the shocked Italian!

No sooner was the ejection seat over the Finish Line than it lost all its horizontal momentum and arced downward, and hit the ground and skidded—on its side—kicking up a million sparks all around Jason, but protecting him with its reinforced construction.

And then it stopped.

A sizzling, steaming crumpled wreck.

Race officials came running from all sides, concerned.

The crowds were stunned into silence.

Henry and Martha Chaser just stared, searching for a sign of life in the smoking ejection seat and the crowd of officials gathering around it.

No one had ever seen anything like it—the kid had *ejected* over the line to win!

And then an official lifted Jason from the crumpled mess of his ejection seat, and Jason stood, wobbling, and held his steering wheel and golden fleece aloft—

—and the roar that went up from the crowd gathered around the Finish Line was like no other that had ever been heard in the history of hover car racing.

It was so loud, it almost brought the city down.

And Henry and Martha Chaser both breathed a sigh

of relief—before Henry leaped into the air, pumping his fists.

"*YOU . . . LITTLE . . . BLOODY . . . BEAUTY!*" he yelled.

Delirious scenes followed.

Like a dam breaking, the ecstatic crowd burst through the barricades and stampeded onto Fifth Avenue, massing around Jason's crumpled ejection seat.

Jason—now flanked by officials and security guards—sought out Alessandro Romba nearby and shook his hand.

"I'm sorry about the Grand Slam, Mr. Romba," Jason said.

Romba just smiled ruefully. "I have a feeling that today might have been my last chance to get it—from now on, I'll be facing a tough new opponent in every race."

Jason nodded. "Good race today."

"You too. Now go, young Chaser. Celebrate."

"I will," Jason smiled broadly.

And he ran off down Fifth Avenue, to the wreck of the *Argonaut*, still lying on its side in the middle of the wide boulevard, where he found the Bug, now standing beside the wreckage.

The two brothers embraced—as camera flashes blazed all around them.

"Jason! Doodlebug!" Martha Chaser came running from the VIP stand, with Henry behind her.

Martha grabbed Jason in a great big hug and squeezed him tight.

Henry Chaser stopped a few steps behind her, knowing that the Bug—currently unhugged—didn't like to be held by him.

He was, then, quite stunned when the Bug leaped up into his arms and cuddled him warmly, resting his head on Henry's shoulder.

"Well *done*, son," Henry said, his voice breaking slightly. "Well *done*."

"Thanks . . . Dad," the Bug whispered softly—the first words he'd ever spoken directly to Henry Chaser.

Martha released Jason. "I almost had a heart attack when your back fin exploded in the final straightaway. What was that all about? Why did that happen?"

"I have an idea," Jason said, turning to see Ariel arrive on the scene, escorted by two New York cops who held between them: Ravi Gupta, the Indian bookmaker, with his hands cuffed.

"Is this him?" one of the cops said to Jason.

"Yeah. That's him," Jason said. "That's the guy who put the explosives on my car in Italy and here."

Both Martha and Henry whirled around. So did all the race officials nearby, leveling their eyes at Gupta.

Jason explained. "I realized it the other night when we saw the gambling odds on TV. In racing, you can bet on all sorts of results: me winning, me coming in the top three overall. But what really caught my attention were the odds for me coming in the top five in any race. And suddenly I thought about the Italian Run.

"Twice in the Italian Run, our team encountered unusual difficulties: that explosion in the home straight-away, but also before that, just before the second pit stop, when Sally was blocked from getting to the Pescara Pits.

"And I realized: In both instances those difficulties arose only when I moved *into fifth place*. On the way to the Pescara Pits, I leapfrogged into fifth by cutting the heel. Then my tailfin exploded just after I got past Trouveau and looked like I would finish in fifth.

"And suddenly I realized: Someone didn't want me to come in in the top five in Italy. So I thought about who that could be . . . and came to one conclusion: gamblers. And there's been only one bookmaker who's shown any interest in me. Gupta.

"So the other night, before I went to bed, I checked his odds on me both here and back in Italy, in particular, Gupta's odds on me coming in the top five in Italy. They were huge. Gupta stood to lose a fortune if I'd come in fifth there, so he'd ensured that I wouldn't: first by blocking

Sally at the Pescara Pits, and second by planting an explosive on my tailfin."

"But how could you prove it?" Henry asked.

"I couldn't. I just had to wait—and see if something similar happened today. So I got Ariel to get some cops to watch Gupta for the whole race and . . ."

He turned to the cop beside Ariel.

The cop said: "We have digital surveillance footage of Mr. Gupta pointing a remote control at the *Argonaut* and pressing a button on that remote a moment before the car's tailfin explodes. Radio-signal surveillance also recorded seek-and-respond signals passing between Gupta's remote and the *Argonaut* an instant before the explosion. Which is why Mr. Gupta is coming with us now."

With that, the cops took Gupta away.

"Gambling . . . ," Sally growled. "It's bad news."

"Oh, it's not that bad," Martha Chaser said daintily.

"And why do you say that, Mom?" Jason asked, surprised.

"Well"—she seemed a little embarrassed to say it—"as I said I would, I put a dollar on you to win the Masters, way back before the first race of the series, when you were at fifteen hundred to one. So I just made fifteen hundred dollars. I think I might get myself that new sewing machine now."

Jason just shook his head and grinned.

And so he was left with his family and his friends and his fleece and the massing, cheering, waving crowd in the middle of Fifth Avenue, New York, on the Sunday of the Masters . . . as the winner.

That same grin was still fixed on his face as he stood on Liberty Island, at the feet of the Statue of Liberty, behind the winner's podium, watching Romba (twenty-six points) and Fabian (twenty-two points, having received no points in Race 4 for crashing) receive their wreaths for coming in second and third in the Masters.

Then came the moment.

"And, now, ladies and gentlemen," the announcer proclaimed, "in first place, with a series total of twenty-eight points, two wins, and one third placing, the Masters Champion for this year... Jason Chaser! Team: *Argonaut*/Lombardi. Navigator: Bug Chaser. Mech Chief: Sally McDuff."

The three of them leaped up onto the podium.

Jason, the Bug, and Sally.

And they accepted their wreaths, and the gigantic Masters Trophy.

Then Jason hefted the enormous trophy aloft, above his head, and the crowd just went ballistic.

And as he looked out over them, Jason thought about everything he'd been through the previous year.

It had, without a doubt, been the most incredible year of his life—a year that had begun in the swamps of Carpentaria, proceeded through the many trials of Race School, and featured an appearance at the Italian Run, before he had finished off the year winning—yes, *winning*—the most prestigious and demanding race series of all: the New York Masters.

And now, to cap it all off, in his pocket sat a contract

from Umberto Lombardi offering him and his team the privilege of racing full-time for the Lombardi Racing Team on the pro circuit next year.

Jason held the trophy high and smiled.

He was Jason Chaser.

Hover car racer.

Jason held the trophy high.